Passing the Bar

Stan Anderson

PublishAmerica
Baltimore

PublishAmerica has allowed this work to remain exactly as the author intended, verbatim, without editorial input.

ISBN: 978-1-4489-6540-3
PUBLISHED BY PUBLISHAMERICA, LLLP
www.publishamerica.com
Baltimore

Printed in the United States of America

Passing the Bar

I sat at the bar sipping my beer. It was my fifth or sixth visit into "Bernie's Bar & Grill". Still new to the area, I sat alone not knowing anyone in the place. It was close to home and the food was decent. I was not here, however, for the food. It was nice if I happened to get hungry as I drank, but drinking was my reason for being here. I spent most of my spare time, which I had lots of, trying to forget my split-up with Flora. I moved out of her house three months prior. I still loved her and she still loved me, but the situation would not allow us to be together. I understood the reason and knew that it was best for everyone involved. Everyone that is, except for me.

The place was dimly lit, which fit my mood perfectly. It, along with the alcohol, also helped unattractive people look a little more attractive. There was a constant murmur of conversation, with an occasional laugh or shout to the bartender for another drink. Music from a local classic rock radio station was piped in throughout. I could hear "Come Sail Away" by "Styx" above the surrounding hum.

I sat alone watching hockey on the big screen. On this particular Wednesday night in January it was the only sport on T.V. Being a huge fan of baseball, football, and basketball I felt as though things were just as they should be for me, since hockey was my only choice for entertainment and I hate hockey. That's the way my life was going at that time. Even though I despised hockey, I thought that it would make me look as if I belonged if I feigned interest in the game—a reason to sit alone and drink myself into a stupor. It was around 8:30 and the bar itself was about three quarters full of drunks varying in age and physical proportions—twelve to fifteen total I would say. Men mostly, but there were three or four women present (I say three or four because there was one I wasn't sure about). People were sitting in groups of two or three, for the most part, talking loudly and laughing. I felt out of place, but I needed to be around people.

Even though they were people I didn't know, or possibly wouldn't even like if I did know. Being alone only reminded me of how fucked up my life had become. At least here I had the luxury of seeing other people whose lives were probably as fucked up, if not more than mine. I had seen the same faces on this night as I had seen on my previous visits. The difference between them and me: They were in packs and I was a rogue, alone and angry.

I watched the game, wondering what the hell was going on, who was playing, and why men on skates were chasing a big round black rubber biscuit around the ice. The end of the period had arrived and the play stopped. I had no choice now but to turn my attention away from the TV. No need to stare at commercials and commentators, especially since there was not any audio coming from the TV. The bartender was a thirty five-ish woman named Joanie. I knew her name well because over the hour or so I had been sitting there I heard her name called out at least eighty times. Sometimes the name came out as "Jeanie" or "Janie", one drunk even called her "Phyllis". Joanie was approximately twenty-five pounds overweight, medium length brown hair pulled back in a pony-tail, wearing a red "Bernie's" t-shirt, and skin tight blue jeans that had most of the men and one of the women drooling on the bar. I, on the other hand, would be afraid to see what and in what direction things would fall once the jeans were removed. Joanie was your typical southern bartender/waitress. She called everyone "hun", or "sweetie". She took care of all the drunks as if they were her own children. And as evidenced by her physique, Joanie had some children of her own. I waved her over to me. She smiled and strutted my way. She knew the old men behind her were admiring her wiggle, and she added a little more "oomph" with every step knowing that her swagger would fill the tip jar.

"You want another half sweetie?" she asked.

"Yeah, one more." I said.

I was drinking beer by the half pitcher. Yes, I know that if you are gonna have two halves, you may as well just order a whole pitcher. But I always kidded myself that I would stop after one……never happened. I was by no means ready to go home and be alone again, so I stayed and drank as long as I could remain upright.

Joanie returned with my beer, "Here ya go hun."

"Thanks" I said.

"Hey, what's your name anyway?" she asked.

"I'm Al" I answered.

"You new around here?" she continued the interrogation, "Don't think I've seen you in here before."

Things at the bar had quieted down since I ordered my first beer, so now Joanie had time to try and improve her tip from me.

"I've been in a few times" I answered "I guess I just haven't been in while you were working."

"No." she said "I would have noticed you." She then gave me a wink.

"I'm Joanie" she said as she walked away, "just yell if ya need me."

Maybe I won't need her anymore. I was on my second half pitcher of beer, had not eaten dinner, and probably should not have a third. Three halves make a whole...lot of beer for one person, especially on an empty stomach. I have to admit that eating was not as high on my priority list as it should have been. I had lost nearly twenty pounds over a three month period. My appetite had disappeared and been replaced with thirst. The good part of that was that I needed to lose the weight and was now exactly where I should be. The bad part was that I still had no appetite and was in danger of becoming a very skinny drunk.

I looked around the bar, and for the first time on this night began noticing the little things around me. I had seen the drunks that were there, but had not really looked at them. On the opposite side of the bar from me were two men, both appeared to be in their fifties. They were dressed nicely and talking quietly as if they were here to discuss business. They were boring, in other words. A few stools to their right were an attractive long-haired blonde, flanked closely on each side by a man with more than bar talk on his mind. The woman was in her late thirties to early forties wearing a very tight, low-cut, light blue sweater that accentuated her God-given (or surgeon-given) assets, large diamond earrings, and perfume that I could detect all the way from across the bar.

The man to her left was thirty-ish, short black hair, wearing a baseball cap and t-shirt. He kept putting his hand on her shoulder as he talked to her and tried to peek down her sweater every time she looked the other way. The man on her right seemed to be a little younger than the other. He was bald, wearing a yellow golf shirt and would put his lips right against her ear as he would talk to her. The woman seemed to be enjoying the attention of both. She was obviously an expert in "Cougarnomics". I was very interested in seeing how this one was going to play out. Was she just toying with these gentlemen for free drinks, with the intention of leaving alone after she had had enough? Would she pick one and leave with him? Would she leave with both? Would the two men leave together hand in hand? Would the men pass out from the fumes of her perfume? I was determined to stay long enough to see the ending.

Immediately to the ménage au trio's right was another trio—a chubby woman, to her right a chubby man, and to his right another man—not so chubby. It appeared as though the chubby man and the chubby woman were husband and wife. The other man was just a friend. All I know is that the two men must have been very good comedians because the chubby woman laughed constantly. And I don't mean "tee hee". Her cackle could be heard above the overhead music, the bar blender, and even through the outer walls of the place. I went outside to smoke earlier and still heard her high pitched hysterics. She did far more than just express amusement and pleasure. Her poor chubby husband must have been terrified to please her in bed for fear of shattering the windows. But from the looks of the two of them, that was probably not a problem.

To my right, at the end of the bar were a man and what I think may have been another man, or possibly a woman....couldn't tell. The two were just talking and enjoying their drinks. There was no evidence of romance, love, affection....or tits. "Obviously a man" was bald, maybe forty-five. The other—uh—person had medium length "Beatles cut" brown hair, was thin and wore a black "Beatles" t-shirt—obviously a "Beatles" fan. As far as the age of "Beatles fan": if I can't guess the gender, good chance I can't guess the age. I listened closely to try and hear the voice, hoping that would help me solve this mystery. As they were talking I leaned over their way to get a napkin from the tray. I was able to hear the voice, but wouldn't ya know it? "Beatles fan" sounded just like Wayne Newton….Danke Schoen. Joanie came down to ask the pair if they wanted another drink. I assumed that she would know them by name since she seemed to know everyone else here by name. She looked at "obviously a man."

"Want another Jack & coke Jim?"

"Yeah, thanks Joanie", said Jim.

Joanie then looked at "Beatles fan". The name will surely give me the answer. I am finally going to find out. Is this a he or a she, a buck or a doe, from Venus or Mars? As Joanie reached out to grab the empty glass from "Beatles fan" she asked

"Another Stoli & tonic Terry?"

DAMMIT!

I guess I'll just have to wait and hope that "Beatles fan", I mean Terry, drinks enough to require a trip to the bathroom. Then I can see which one he/she enters.

The rest of the crowd was on my side of the bar and I didn't have a very good look at them. All of the "Bernie's" patrons were seated at the bar. The tables and booths that surrounded the bar were empty. The elongated oval shaped bar sat in the middle of a large room. On each of the long sides, booths lined the walls about six feet from the bar. At the front were seven or eight high-top tables designed to seat four or five each. At the back of the room was a small, twelve by fifteen, stage raised only about a foot above the floor. In front of the stage on each side was a table large enough to accommodate larger groups. Between these two tables was the tiny dance floor. The dance floor was nothing more than a bare spot in the room. On the walls around the entire room were all sorts of NASCAR memorabilia. There were pictures, plaques, encased articles of clothing identified with a number, a large banner with the entire year's race schedule, and hanging from the ceiling near the front door was a plastic replica of a car. The car was approximately 8' long and 4' wide. It was covered with the traditional decals advertising everything from insurance to laundry detergent. It looked as though the car was red underneath all the decals. The number "98" was on the side of the car, which meant nothing to me since I am not a NASCAR fan either. NASCAR fans have the reputation of being uneducated, poor white trash rednecks. As soon as I have evidence to dispute this theory I will no longer stand by it. As far as the plastic car, I tried to never walk directly underneath it because it appeared to be supported by very thin fishing line and duct tape. On each end of the room was a row of T.V.s lined up high on the walls. Both sides had a large screen in the center with two smaller screens on each side. It appeared that the NASCAR fans and all other sports fans could be entertained at any given time. I'm sure that the big screens, however, were reserved on race days. Thankfully the music that was piped in was "classic rock" and not "country &western."

Three of my previous visits to "Bernie's" had been on weekends. The small stage and dance floor are used on Friday and Saturday nights. Live bands show up on these nights—your basic three or four person group that recently got up the courage to leave the basement or garage and actually thought they deserved to be heard in public. Since a different band plays every weekend, I had been privileged to see and hear three different bands. The average male member of these bands had gray hair, a potbelly, and needed a breather after only a few songs. I, for one, welcomed the breaks. One band had a female singer. She wore a tank top to show off all of her tattoos. The problem was she should have been wearing an overcoat to cover herself all over. The musical talents of all the bands ranged from covers of "Lynyrd Skynyrd" all the way to "The Allman Brothers"—very talented people.

Beside me at the bar I was able to overhear a conversation

between two men. One wore a shirt and tie, the other blue jeans and a denim jacket. I had heard Joanie earlier refer to the denim wearer as "Phil" and the other as "Don". Phil resembled "Barney Fife" and Don looked like an older version of "Arnold Horshack."

"John Holmes was a bigger star than Ron Jeremy", said Phil.

"No way" said Don, "Anyone who has ever seen porn knows Ron Jeremy. Not everyone knows John Holmes. Jeremy was a bigger star"

These two were definitely a couple of winners. Together they combined to make an eighty-year-old virgin. These two would be considered nerds by "trekkies". With the names, Phil and Don (same first names as the "Everly Brothers"), I decided that if I ever had to refer to this pair by name they would be the "Neverlaid Brothers". They obviously knew their porn, however.

"We'll ask Joanie." said Phil, "Hey Joanie, who was bigger, John Holmes or Ron Jeremy?"

Joanie, who was bent over the sink washing glasses didn't even look up as she said, "I don't remember I was too drunk. I just know I was sore as hell the next day."

My name is Al Saunders. I drink too much, have a crappy job and am poison when it comes to relationships with women. I am 48-years-old and I don't know what I want to be when I grow up. Hopefully I'll find out before my liver explodes. The hockey game is starting up. I don't want to miss any of the riveting action.

By the way: The cougar left with both men, but both men came back inside shortly thereafter. The rejection obviously occurred at the car door. Terry entered the men's room, but I was further confused when Jim entered the lady's.

~

Flora and I met a little over a year and a half ago. She and her husband had recently divorced. I, at the time, was living with my parents. Yes, I was living with my parents. I had lost my house in a recent divorce and needed someplace to stay in a hurry. Thankfully, Mom & Dad kept the nest open for me to return temporarily. It was cramped and uncomfortable, but on the positive side I had a never-ending supply of "Preparation H" and "Geritol" at my disposal. Since there was only one TV, I did a lot of reading in my room. You can take only so much "Wheel of Fortune" and "Little House on the Prairie" reruns. But I cannot complain. I had a roof over my head and Momma's cooking every night.

I was at McDonald's on a Saturday afternoon with my son, Michael. It was a cloudy June day in Constance, GA. We had just finished our cheeseburgers and Michael was enjoying the indoor playground. There were kids running around the playground equipment screaming and laughing without regard to anything or anyone around them......kids being kids in other words. My patience, however, for this type of ruckus is usually quite low.

After my table has been bumped by some snot-nosed brat for the tenth time I am usually ready to leave, no matter how hard Michael pleads to stay "five more minutes". As I sucked on my leftover "Dr. Pepper" I couldn't even sit it on the table, knowing that if I did it would end up on my shirt or in my lap. It appeared to me that the parents who were suppose to be watching these kids were not even around. I wanted to prove to myself that they weren't around. I did a quick count of the kids. Some were not visible in the tower of tubes and slides, but I deduced that there were probably 18 to 20 kids present. I then began to look to the tables around the playground to count adults. As I was all the way up to 4 adults across the room I looked to the tables beside me.... and there she was. She was two tables down from me sitting alone, watching the kids. She must have sensed that I was looking her way because she immediately turned, looked straight at me and smiled. The most beautiful smile I had ever witnessed. It was a smile that exuded love. I was embarrassed at first and then amazed by her smile. When I finally realized that I was just staring at her I was able to force a smile toward her. Still smiling, she refocused her attention to the kids. I took her look toward me and the smile to mean that she was interested in talking to me (I didn't know it at the time, but I could have been a hunchback Cyclops with facial warts and a bad toupee' and I would have gotten the same loving smile. That was Flora.)

I got up from my table and boldly walked over to her table.

"Can I buy you a drink?" I asked, "Sprite, Dr. Pepper, Hi-C Lemonade?"

What a cheesy way to introduce myself. Actually I hadn't introduced myself at all, just made an ass of myself. Maybe next I should ask her to dance to the McDonald's "elevator music". I looked at her expecting to be politely shot down. After seeing her up close and peering into her gorgeous green eyes I knew this woman was way out of my league. But she laughed at my lame come-on and said, "Ya know what? I would love a refill on my diet coke".

Her voice was as beautiful as her face, a genteel southern accent that made me proud to be Georgia boy. She had shoulder length dirty blonde wavy hair, smooth dark complexion, very little makeup, and did I mention her smile? If I had to guess her age, I would say 39. She had a look of experience and youthful enthusiasm.

"Sure" I said.

I then rushed to the counter to get her refill. What am I going to say next to ruin my chances with her? I had always prided myself in my ability to talk to women, but she had me as nervous as a Tourette's patient at a Baptist revival. Was I just out of practice? I had not dated since my divorce, and not tried to ask anyone out in over nine years. But as I returned to her table and handed her the drink she bailed me out.

"Thank you so much... My name's Flora"

"Hi" I was able to stammer out, "I'm Al"

"So do you have a kid here or do you just stalk out the McDonald's playground for single moms?" She was still smiling.

I looked around, hoping he was in view.

"That's mine" I said as I pointed out Michael in the ball pit.

"Mine aren't visible right now. They're up in that big thing." She pointed to the tower of tubes and slides.

"How many do you have?" I asked.

"Two. My son, Kyle is six and my daughter, Taylor is nine." She's still smiling.

"Have a seat" she said as she motioned to the opposite side of the table, "How old is your son?"

"Michael is seven." I answered as I obeyed and sat.

"Michael? Really?" she asked, "My grandmother wanted

Kyle's name to be Michael. She was a big believer that angels were always with us and around to protect us if we asked.

So she wanted me to name her great grandson after Archangel Michael. Is that where you got the name?"

"No" I said, "My ex wife was a big Michael Jackson fan."

Her smile turned into a laugh. Yes, her laugh was beautiful too.

"Why didn't you name your son Michael?" I asked.

"My ex, Raymond, and I had already decided to name Kyle after Raymond's maternal grandfather and my father. So my son's name is Robert Kyle."

She said ex. That means no husband. I figured that to be the case, but now I know. Thank you, God.

"Your father's name is Robert?" I asked.

"Yes, and Raymond's grandfather's full name was Robert Kyle. We named our daughter Taylor. That was my mom's maiden name. Sometimes people hear her name and think she's a boy. I have to correct them often and let them know that Taylor is all girl."

"No. Taylor has been a unisex name for a while now. Flora's a unique name…very pretty but unique. Is it a family name?"

"No. My mother loves flowers." She answered "They are everywhere in and around her house. I keep telling her that they're gonna eventually gobble her up, there are so many. And some are so big. Anyway, she said that when the nurse first handed me to her a few days after I was born, she looked at me and then at all the beautiful flowers that were in her room, sent by family and friends. She said that I was much prettier than any of the flowers, but I just seemed to belong in the midst of all that beauty. She named me "Flora" after the Roman goddess of flowers. Her and my dad had already decided on a name, but when she saw me the name they picked went out the window. I know I sound arrogant telling you how pretty my mother said I was as a baby, but I'm just retelling the story I have heard a thousand times."

"You don't sound arrogant at all" I said, "Why did your mother not see you for several days after you were born?

"I was fine. I was perfectly healthy, but my mother had massive internal bleeding and was in ICU for several days after I was born. That, I think, had a lot to do with her love for flowers now. When she was finally clear of danger, removed from ICU and into a normal room, "the entire space except for the bed" as she put it, was filled with flowers. The flowers in her room signified life—her life which was now no longer in danger, and my life—her first child whom she was about to meet."

"Okay, I gotta ask. What was your name gonna be?"

"Helen Lucille" she winced.

"Okay Lucy, I won't comment on that. What is your middle name?"

"Don't have one" she said, "Mom says goddesses only have one name."

She then laughed at her previous statement and said, "I'm sorry that's my mom talking again. I'm really not arrogant."

"Not arrogant" I said. "But apparently adored by your mother."

"Yes. Still to this day."

"Your mom and dad still together?"

"No" she said, "They divorced when I was a toddler. My dad lives in Florida….been re-married twice. He's currently on his second. My mom re-married when I was twelve….still married to the same man. That's enough about me Al, what do you do?"

I didn't want to answer. Her life seemed so interesting, I was afraid I was going to bore her with any details about mine.

"I work at 'Merchants Lumber'. I fill orders for builders, contractors and the like. I'm called a salesman, but for the most part I'm just an order taker."

"You off every weekend?" she asked

"Yeah. That's one of the good things about my job—no nights, weekends or holidays. What about you? What do you do?"

"I'm a veterinarian. My mom loves vegetation. I love animals."

"You treat all animals?" I asked.

"I wouldn't say all. Mostly dogs and cats of course. I routinely care for an opossum, a parrot, several ferrets, a deer, and some goats, just to name a few. But if someone brings in a snake I politely ask them to take it somewhere else."

"Ever have to give mouth to mouth?" I joked.

"Actually," she answered, "It didn't happen at work, but I was visiting one of my friends a while back and she had some kittens outside on her patio. They were only a few days old. One of the kittens wandered away and fell in her pool. Taylor was outside and found the kitten floating in the pool. She started screaming, so I ran out and found Taylor in the pool fishing out the kitten. It was February. Long story short—cat is now alive and well. So to answer your question—yes."

"Wow!" I said. "You actually gave a kitten mouth to mouth?"

"It had drowned and my daughter went into a frigidly cold pool on a frigidly cold day to try and save it, so yes."

Flora was still smiling. I was starting to think that it was permanent and she was incapable of expressing anything but happiness.

"How long you been divorced?" I asked her.

"Not final yet. But it is as far as I'm concerned. We split up three months ago right after I filed. It'll be a couple more months til its final."

"How long you been divorced?" she asked.

"Split up a year ago, divorce was final six months ago. How long were you married?"

"16 years" she said, "He wasn't unfaithful, He wasn't abusive and I still love him. I just couldn't stand to be around him anymore, and he felt the same way about me."

How could anyone not want to be around this beautiful babe?

"16 years. That's gotta be tough." I said, "Mine lasted half that long and that was tough enough for me."

"It's definitely not easy, especially when you have to explain everything that's going on to the kids, but when you both know that it's time, the decision isn't so difficult."

"You live close by?' I asked.

"Not far, maybe three miles. I got to keep the house, which was good. We had only lived there 8 months when we separated. You live close by?"

How am I gonna answer this? I might as well be honest now. If anything comes of this, she will want to see where I live eventually.

"Yes, I live only a couple of miles from here......with my parents."

She didn't blink. She kept her seat. She did not abruptly tell me she had to leave. Instead she made feel comfortable with the situation.

"It's nice to have family close by. I've had to do the same thing myself more than once."

We sat at the table in the McDonald's playground area for an hour and a half talking about anything and everything......important to trivial, interesting to boring. It was all important and interesting to me because I was engaged in a conversation with a beautiful woman who seemed to be genuinely interested in me as well. We learned a lot about each other in that time. Even though we were learning about each other, the conversation flowed as if we had known each other forever. All three children, at some time, individually came to us to ask when we were leaving. Flora and I actually outlasted the children at the McDonald's playground. Eventually the children got to know each other and started playing together. Michael was not yet into girls, but he accepted Taylor because she was Kyle's sister.

As the time to say goodbye arrived I was sorry to have to end our conversation. Flora seemed sad about it too. I hoped this split up would be temporary. She stood up, and for the first time I saw her standing. I was not at all disappointed. Flora stands 5'2" and is very well proportioned. Not petit, not big, but nice and curvy. If I had to compare her figure to someone it would be Marilyn Monroe. Yeah, I could do a lot worse. I was feeling much more comfortable with her now and had no trouble asking, "Can I give you a call? Maybe go out for drinks sometime?"

"Yeah, I would like that." she said.

She gave me her cell phone number, and I gave her mine.

"Okay. It was a real pleasure meeting you." The kids were standing right there with us and even though I wanted to kiss her and squeeze her until her green eyes popped out of her head to show how much of a pleasure it really was, that was the best I could do.

"Nice meeting you too, Al. Bye Michael, it was nice meeting you" She walked away and out the door with her kids.

I had promised Michael that we would see a movie after lunch. Fortunately for us, the movie was a popular one and was showing at the theater on several different screens every forty minutes or so. The extra time we had spent at McDonald's was no big deal. What movie did we see? I have no clue. I was thinking about Flora. She was the only thing on my mind. I sat in a dark theater for two hours and had absolutely no idea what I had seen. The only image I saw was her as she walked away from us that afternoon. The important thing though, is that Michael enjoyed the movie.

~

The next morning I woke up at around 8:30. I knew that Michael would be asleep at least another hour or so. I ate a bowl of cereal and watched Sport Center on ESPN. My parents were up and outside doing whatever eighty-year-old people do at 8:30 on Sunday morning. I think they were checking the garden for okra, green beans, watermelons or something else you could easily pick up at the store. I still had Flora on my mind. I wanted to call her right away, but this early on Sunday morning would probably earn me demerits with her. I needed to find something to keep me busy until I thought it was safe to call her. I started feeling guilty because I would be taking my son home later that day to his mom, and all I could think about was a woman I hardly knew. I decided that Michael and I would do something fun today after he got up and had breakfast. That way my mind would be away from her and I would have some quality time with my son.

Michael got up at almost 10:00. I was still in front of the T.V. when he walked into the living room. He was wearing blue shorts and a "Sponge Bob Square Pants" t-shirt. He always slept with
• Sponge Bob.

"Mornin' Dad."

Michael was a little undersized for his age. Not much, but he was smaller than most of his classmates. I had noticed yesterday that Kyle, Flora's six-year-old, was one to two inches taller than Michael. At seven, size matters, especially for boys. There aren't a lot of popular short, skinny boys in the second grade.

"Hey sport. Whatcha wanna do today?"

"Watch T.V.…. What's for breakfast?"

He wanted to watch TV?

"Tell me what you want and I'll see if we have it."

He focused his eyes upward as if the answer was on the ceiling.

"Pancakes and bacon" he decided.

"Okay" I said, "You sure you don't wanna do anything today other than watch TV?"

"I'm sure. There's a show on today that I wanna watch."

I could have insisted that Michael do something other than watch TV today, but the split up between his mother and I had been very rough on him. He was just starting to get adjusted to the every other weekend thing with me, and I did not want to add to his distress by making him do something he didn't want to do. I wanted his life to be as trouble-free as possible. If he wants to watch TV all day, I'll let him, for now. I went to the kitchen and fetched my boy some pancakes and bacon. Frozen pancakes and microwave bacon is ready in less than three minutes. Michael ate it in less than two. I normally enjoyed cooking the real thing, but here in my parent's house I tried to disturb as little as possible.

My parents came inside and got ready for church. A couple that lives up the street, older than me but younger than my folks, pick them up and take them every Sunday. My mom did her best to make me feel bad about not taking Michael to church before she left.

"He needs to be going to Sunday school and learning about Jesus. You should be going too. Couldn't do you any harm."

My dad, standing behind her, gave me a look—his eyes saying, "Listen to your mother."

I listened respectively, nodded and said "Maybe next time."

I had no intention of forcing religion on my son. If he wants to go to church I certainly won't stop him. But I refuse to force him to believe something just because others believe it, the way it was forced on me. After Jim and Tammy Faye left, Michael and I perched ourselves in front of the television for hours of Sponge Bob, Drake & Josh, iCarly, and Chowder. I fell asleep during the first show and woke up at 12:30.

Even though I had felt very comfortable with Flora when I had left her the day before, I was getting nervous about calling her. Things between us just seemed to click so effortlessly that it appeared to be too perfect.

Did she give me her number just to be nice, with no intention of answering when I called? Was she just ready to go and gave me her number to get rid of me? What if it's a fake number?

"Hello?"

"Hi… Flora? This is Al. We met yesterday at Mc…"

"Yes Al." she interrupted, "I haven't forgotten you yet. How are you?"

"I'm good. Hey, I am taking Michael back to his mother's tonight and I was wondering if you would like to get together afterward?"

"I would love to if I can find someone to stay with the kids. What time were you thinking?"

"Around 7:30. Is that good?"

"It's good as long as I can find a kid-sitter. I can't say baby-sitter any more it pisses the kids off"

"Okay. We have a few hours, just let me know if you can."

"I'll probably be able to find someone." She said, "There are three teenagers that live nearby who I can trust. What time will you leave to take Michael to his mom's?"

"Around 5:30."

"Okay. I will let you know something before then."

"Okay. Bye."

"Bye."

Now I'm anxious. I could be waiting for four hours to get an answer. How hard is she going to be looking for someone to stay with the kids? She sounded genuinely happy to hear from me and excited about the idea of getting together. But I have been in this place so many times, that I know not to make any assumptions. I barely know her, and although she seems perfect, I have got to be careful. A lot of women run hot and cold, just like a shower. I know from lots of experience, that there is a very good chance, I'm either going to get burned or need to have my heart amputated due to frost-bite.

My phone is ringing…. It's her.

"Hello?"

I knew it was her, but it was too soon to give her a "Hey" or "That was quick" as I answered.

"Hey. I found a sitter."

It had been less than five minutes. I guess she was actually excited to do something with me.

"Great. Want to meet somewhere or you want me to pick you up?"

"Call me after you drop off Michael and we'll arrange a place to meet."

"Okay. Talk to ya then."

I'll let go of the paranoia for now. I'm sure it will creep back in later.

Here it comes….Why does she want me to meet her somewhere? Does she not want me to know where she lives?

Okay, I'm really letting go of it this time.

What do I wear? I was wearing dark green cargo shorts, a white "Elvis Costello" t-shirt, and flip flops when we met. I wanted to exhibit a bit more fashion taste tonight without over doing it. Jeans? No, too hot. Dockers? No, too dressy. Overalls? No. I decided on a pair of khaki shorts and a dark blue golf shirt. I have to admit I have been complimented on my blue eyes throughout my entire life. I thought that the blue shirt would help bring attention to them. I wore white bootie socks and white Nike's. Wearing sneakers, I decided, would help me to appear more athletic.

~

After dropping Michael off at his mom's, I arrived at "Ricky's Tavern" precisely at 7:30, our arranged meeting time. Flora had mentioned it as a place that had a nice atmosphere and pretty good food. I had never been. As I found a parking space I looked to my left and saw that Flora had arrived as well. She was parked a few spaces away from me, still sitting in her car. She had not noticed me so I got out of my truck and walked over to her door. I saw that she was on her phone. She looked up, saw me, smiled and opened her door. As she got out of her car she finished her conversation with, "He's here. Talk to you tomorrow."

"Hi." She said, "That was my friend, Kathy. I called her while I was waiting for you because after I got here I started feeling really nervous. I just realized that I have not had a 'date' in eighteen years. I needed someone to talk me into staying."

"Thanks a lot."

"No. It should make you feel good that I'm nervous. I wouldn't care if I didn't like you. I wasn't really gonna leave."

I couldn't wait. This was our first encounter away from the kids. Her smile was still there, she wore a little more makeup than she had the day before. I didn't think it possible but even though she didn't require makeup, her green eyes shown brighter than I had remembered because of it (She purposely brought attention to her eyes too. How vain can you get?). Her hair was pulled back on each side and held in place by red flower barrettes, allowing her beautiful face to be in full view (This "Babe" was nervous about meeting me on a date?), Her silver 'spaghetti strap' blouse and black Capri pants hugged her body as if they were made specifically for her on this particular day. Her black open-toed leather shoes were flat, no heels. I couldn't wait. She smelled like flowers—not perfume, not lotion, not Irish Spring—real flowers. Flora was indeed the goddess of flowers. Their aromas followed her. I couldn't wait. We had known each other for approximately 31 hours and had never touched. No hello handshake, no obligatory goodbye hug, not even a purposeful accidental brush against one another. That would have probably been different had there been no kids around. I couldn't wait. As we still stood next to her car I faced her, looked down into her emerald eyes, put my left hand around her and on her back, pulled her to me and kissed her. She kissed back…and very well I will say. I put my right hand on the back of her neck, pulling her toward me even though she could get no closer. She put her arms around me and with her hands on my shoulder blades, pulled me toward her, although I could get no closer. The kiss lasted for what seemed to be three seconds, but was probably more like two minutes. After we pulled away, we stared into each other's eyes for a moment and then walked into the restaurant.

Inside the restaurant we sat at a booth—both of us on the same side. Flora ordered a rum & sprite, I ordered a vodka & tonic. Neither of us was very hungry so we split a stuffed mushroom appetizer. As we sat there I did not notice anything about the establishment we were in. I was dialed in to Flora. We didn't talk much. I guess the kiss we had had outside was all the conversation we needed for a while. We mostly just looked at each other, smiled, and pecked each other on the lips between bites and sips. The appetizer was half-eaten, two additional drinks each had been ordered and emptied when we decided it was time to leave. It was 8:35. We walked outside and I escorted her to her car. I knew that the evening was not nearly over, but I didn't want to seem presumptuous.

"What time do you have to be home for the baby-sitter?" I asked as we stood next to her car.

"I didn't really know what to tell her so I said I would call her. I do know that she has to be back home by midnight though."

"Do you wanna call her and tell her you will be home at 11:30?" I asked with my fingers crossed on one hand and rubbing her shoulder with the other.

Her ever-present smile was then accompanied by an evil twinkle in her eyes.

"Okay. Give me a minute."

I wanted to jump up and give the world a fist bump. But I kept myself composed as she got into her car, closed the door and punched numbers into her cell phone. She talked for what seemed to be hours. Is there an emergency? Does she have to get home right away? Did the baby-sitter put aluminum foil in the microwave? I was starting to panic when she opened the car door and got out.

"I have permission to stay out a little longer. Kyle needed some convincing but he said it was okay."

"We'll take my truck" I said.

"Where are we going?" She asked, even though she knew what was on both of our minds.

"Don't know yet. I'm just not ready to tell you "goodnight."

She had kids and a baby-sitter at home.

I had parents at home. But only two short blocks up the road was the "Kumon Inn". It was not a five-star facility, but it was clean enough for what was on our dirty minds. I parked and went in to get a room while Flora waited in the truck. Standing behind the counter was Fusari. I knew this because she was wearing a name tag.

"How many in your party?" she asked.

"Two."

"Will you be wanting two doubles or one king?"

"A king."

"Smoking or non-smoking?"

"Smoking."

"How many key cards will you be needing?"

"One."

"Top floor or bottom floor?"

Jeez! Am I going to have a choice in the drapery pattern too?

"Bottom" I said.

Fusari punched the vital stats into her computer and waited for a response.

"I am so sorry sir to tell you that we do not have a king bed, smoking room on the bottom floor. I can offer you smoking with queen beds on the bottom floor, smoking with king bed on the top floor, non-smoking with king bed on the bottom floor, or I can call our sister facility in Macon to see if they may be able to accommodate you."

"That won't be necessary," I said through clinched teeth, knowing that time was valuable. I pointed to the side door of the lobby which was directly in front of my truck outside.

"Just give me the room that is closest to that door please."

"That would be room #112, non-smoking, king bed on the bottom floor."

"Perfect."

I signed the slip she handed me without even looking at it. She gave me the key card and I left the desk. There were no other cars in the parking lot. It was Sunday night. The entire hotel had to be vacant. I'll bet they don't even have a king bed, smoking room on the bottom floor. Not that the details of the room were that important to me, the problem was I just wasted ten minutes of potential undisturbed alone time with Flora to find that out.

I walked quickly to the side door I had pointed out to Fusari, opened it and waved Flora inside. She got out and walked quickly toward me as I held the door open for her. I locked the truck with a beep from my key fob and closed the door behind us. We were like two teenagers after the prom. Only a few steps from the door we entered room #112, king bed, no smoking (I'm smoking anyway), and an awful drapery pattern. If this had been a one-night stand or a meaningless fling I may have provided juicy details here. But it was Flora and me, and I refuse to speak of her in any lurid tone. All I will say is, after two hours and twenty-two minutes, I cursed time for existing. Neither of us wanted the evening to end. And even though we knew it had to end, we wished that it could end by saying "goodnight" and then holding each other as we fell asleep.

Flora and I began to see each other on a regular basis—every night on the weekend, and at least once during the week I would go to her house for dinner. Her kids were with their dad on the same weekends that Michael was with his mom. This gave us every other weekend alone without kids. Those weekends were spent without clothing for the most part. I enjoyed spending time with Flora and after only a couple of weeks I could tell that she was starting to have strong feelings for me. She even told me that she was getting scared because she thought she was falling hard for me. All I could say was "Don't". I was having the same feelings, but I was horrified at the thought of getting hurt again. This pattern has followed me my entire adult life:

1—I actually remain with the same woman for over a month
2—Woman falls madly in love with me
3—I act uninterested
4—Woman falls deeper in love me
5—I give in and realize I love her too
6—We decide to get married/live together
7—Woman drops me like rat turd mistaken for a raisin
8—I go temporarily insane

Things started no differently for Flora and me.

She treated me as if I was the most important and precious human on earth. I followed the pattern exactly acting not so interested in her, even cold and rude at times. I tried to balance my icy times with occasional acts or words of love and affection. I didn't want to lose her. I just wanted to plant a seed of doubt as to my worthiness for her as a long-termer. I don't want to imply that I was a total asshole to Flora. I just did not allow my true feelings for her to come forward. When she would sit next to me on the couch and snuggle next to me I would put my arm around her, but I wouldn't put my arm around her so that she would snuggle next to me. I knew deep down that Flora made me happy and was much more than worthy for me, but I had to protect my heart. The bottom line is I couldn't bear the thought of losing her. But no way could I bear the devastation of loving her and losing her.

After four months together Flora and I planned a long weekend trip to Hilton Head Island. It was, of course, our weekend without kids and Flora arranged for her sister to keep Kyle and Taylor on Thursday and Friday so that we could have an extended weekend. It was our first trip away together and we were both excited to get away and have no distractions. I, of course, didn't act quite so excited. I had to keep my relaxed and laid-back attitude toward our relationship. We spent the first two days on the beach, splitting time between lying in a lounge chair, wading into the ocean, and walking along the shore. Needless to say we both turned bright red from sunburn. That wasn't so bad, however, because it allowed us to rub each other down from head to toe with lotion every evening in the hotel room. We even rubbed the areas that were not burned. The hotel room was much nicer than the one at "Kumon Inn", king bed, third floor with a gorgeous view of the ocean, smoking, and a nice drapery pattern. We made love in the morning, in the afternoon, in the evening and in the middle of the night with no concern of who could hear our grunts and moans of pleasure (some of the grunts and moans were from sunburn pain, but it was mostly pleasure). When we woke up on the morning of our third day there, we knew that the smart thing for us to do was stay inside to avoid further frying of the skin.

But you do not vacation at the beach to hang out in the hotel room. We covered ourselves in SPF 50 and returned to the white sand.

That evening we had a wonderful seafood dinner at a restaurant called "The Flying Fin", which was located at the end of a pier, out over the ocean. The restaurant logo was a blue marlin soaring over a blue sea. We split a dozen raw oysters. I had steak and crab legs, Flora had shrimp scampi. She helped me finish the crab legs. After dinner and two bottles of chardonnay we sipped on cognac as we stared at the ocean from the restaurant patio. Leaning over the rail directly above the crashing waves below, I could think of no other place I wanted to be or anyone else I wanted to be with—another evening with Flora that I did not want to end. But I still acted cool. We finished our drinks, left the pier, and instead of returning to the car, we took off our shoes and walked along the shoreline letting the tiny waves trickle along our bare feet. The ocean breeze was the perfect tonic for our burnt skin. We had driven to the restaurant from our hotel, but the night was so beautiful that we decided to walk the mile and a half to the hotel and return for her car in the morning. Hope it doesn't rain.

On our return to the hotel, we walked by the pool and over to the tiki bar which was now closed. We each sat on a bar stool and looked up at the stars not wanting to go in just yet.

"Aren't the stars beautiful?" she asked.

"Yeah. Sky's full of 'em tonight."

Still protecting myself, I did not want to cave to the moment. I did not want to face my feelings for Flora. She's too perfect. I'm not good enough for her and one day she will realize that.

"This trip has been so amazing Al. I'm already planning the next one in my head."

"Yeah, me too."

"Okay, when?" She asked with wide eyes.

"It's October. It'll be getting too cold soon—hafta be next year—maybe May."

"I don't know if I can wait that long. Let's go somewhere else, where it's always warm, like Key West." Her hands were clasped together as if she was pleading.

"That's a long drive—hafta be more than a long weekend."

"We'll fly." She said excitedly with a tiny jump off her seat.

"Okay, but that trip's gotta be on you. I can't afford that."

I was struggling to keep my cool, nonchalant demeanor. I was ecstatic inside to hear her talk about more trips, future plans.

"Fine, I'll get on the internet when I get home and look into it." She said as she leaned back against the bar.

"Just let me know what you plan so I make sure I can get off work."

Then there was silence. I looked at Flora as she was leaning back with her elbows on the bar, staring at the sky. She was still holding her sandals, dangling from her fingers as she rhythmically swayed them back and forth. She sat with her smooth pink legs crossed, wearing tan short shorts and a tight dark brown tank top that showed off her Marilyn Monroe figure. Her hair was slightly mussed from the breeze, her barrettes which were holding it back earlier had been put away. As mundane as the description may seem, she was stunning. It was Flora—casually dressed, perfectly relaxed, gorgeous even though her hair was a little ruffled. It was a sight that I knew would be etched in my mind forever............ I love her. I can't deny it any more. I LOVE HER! My charade has got to end. She has to know how I feel. I got up off my stool and walked over to her. She took her focus off the sky and looked at me—smiling of course. As I stood in front of her she uncrossed her legs and leaned toward me. Her smile disappeared after she looked at me closer. I had not realized it until that moment, but my eyes were watery and tears were rolling down my cheeks.

"What's wrong?" she asked with a worried look.

I couldn't talk. I knew my voice would break if I tried to speak, so I took a second to compose myself.

"Al! What's wrong? You're scaring me."

"I...."

I took a deep breath and wiped my face.... two more deep breaths. Flora continued to look at me anxiously.

"I love you, Flora."

Sandals fell to the ground. The concern on her face disappeared and quickly turned into delight. She jumped off her stool and squeezed me as I squeezed back.

"I love you Al." she said as she wiped away her own tears, "I didn't think you were ever gonna say it."

After this enlightenment I became a changed man. Flora was no longer "Flora" to me. She became "honey," "baby," "sweetie," and every other vomit-inducing term of endearment you could think of. Cool, calm, and indifferent transformed into affectionate, caring, doting, and more amorous than ever (amorous had never been a problem). No longer was she someone for me to try and push away, she became my reason for breathing. Her smile turned me into a slobbering tail-wagging puppy.

Flora, however, didn't change at all. She remained a kind, gentle, and loving angel. She made me feel as if I was her reason for breathing. My life away from Flora improved as well. I was happy. Work went much smoother. My clients, all of a sudden, were easier to deal with. Even strangers I would encounter in passing would say hello, smile, or just give a friendly nod. I was madly in love and love emanated from me and into the world.

Shortly after our beach trip, Flora asked me to move in with her. The decision was tough. But as much as I enjoyed living with my eighty-year-old parents and the constant smell of "Vicks VapoRub" and prune juice, I accepted. After I moved in, we were like honeymooners. We already made love as if we both had been in prison for the previous five years. But it was surprisingly better now. We were sickeningly in love, and I was not afraid. This one is going to last forever.

~

Although Flora and I couldn't have been happier together, the blending of kids with kids and adults with kids wasn't so smooth. Kyle and Taylor were very good, well mannered kids.

But when Flora and I first started dating neither child liked me at all. They would avoid me if I was visiting by staying in their rooms, or asking their mom if they could go to a friend's house. At times when Flora and I planned dinner out with the kids, they would beg out of going and ask if we could grab something "to go" for them. Their daddy had not been gone from the house that long, and they were not ready for a "daddy figure". As time passed, their coldness toward me decreased a little at a time. I love these kids as if they were mine, and did all I could to try and win them over. They were eventually able to tolerate me being with their mom and accepted me as an adult friend. Michael was also new to them and at first Kyle enjoyed having someone new to play with, as did Michael. Kyle even asked Michael to spend the night with him at least once every time I had Michael with me. Michael seemed to like Flora from the beginning just as I had. Taylor, of course, just saw Michael as a little boy and a nuisance, just as any preteen girl would. And at seven, Michael hated girls...eeeeww. Their dog, Scratch, loved both Michael and me from the beginning. Scratch, an eight pound ball of matted fur, was a mutt that loved everyone though. He quickly became an ally to me.

But after I moved in, the relationship between Flora's children and me went backward. The effort all of us, including the kids, had put into making our connection work seemed to have been wasted. I was now taking up much more of their mommy's time. The way the kids saw it, there was a war between them and me for mommy's attention & affection and I seemed to be winning. Not having the attention from their mom that they craved only intensified their distress of not having their daddy around. The fact that I was now occupying the space that he once occupied, slept in the bed where he once slept, mowed the lawn that he once mowed, told them goodnight face to face every night while he couldn't, made them resent me terribly. Who could blame them? Michael seemed to be happy with his every other weekend home, but he also was not warm to the fact that Flora was replacing his mother as Daddy's companion. The difference was that Michael did not have an everyday reminder of this situation and Flora's children did.

The clash also affected the children's relationships with each other. They saw one another as the baggage that came along with the corresponding adult. On the weekends I had Michael all the kids would keep to themselves and have very little interaction. Blinded by the severity of the disconnection between the children and us, Flora and I continued to enjoy our lives together.

The trip to Key West never happened, but Flora was not disappointed. She was happy, just as I was that we were living together and enjoying every day being with one another. She hated to cook, I loved to cook. She loved yard work, I hated yard work. We both hated cleaning the house, so we shared the duties. It wasn't Key West but we did take other trips. We spent a week with all the kids in tow in Panama City Beach the following summer. Flora's Dad and step mom lived nearby and we were able to spend a lot of time with them as well. The two of us also returned to Hilton Head that same summer for another long weekend. The following October, a year after our first beach trip, we planned a weekend getaway to the north Georgia mountains—just the two of us in a cabin, with lots of alone time. We were looking forward to the moonlit walks, outdoor Jacuzzi, and all the beautiful sights of a mountain autumn. Flora had taken most of that Friday off to finish preparing for our trip. Her ex-husband, Raymond, would be picking up Kyle and Taylor that afternoon. As I was driving home from work I got a call from Flora.

"Honey, where are you?" She was noticeably upset. I could tell she had been crying.

"I'm still about twenty minutes away." I said "What's wrong?"

"Just hurry home. I have to talk to you."

She had me scared.

"Everyone is fine" she said, "Be careful, but get home as quick as you can."

"What is it?"

"I'm sorry. I don't want to talk about this on the phone. Please hurry, Honey…I love you."

"I love you too."

I had seen Flora cry before, but not that often. She cried when I first told her I loved her, and she cried after watching a couple of movies—I remember one of them was "The Notebook". She said everyone is fine, so I knew the kids were okay. My mind was wandering in every different direction. What could it be? Did something happen at work? Was it Scratch? Did the house burn down? Did Angelina and Brad break up? What could it be?

Of course on my way home I got behind every geriatric driver on the highway that day. I hit every red light and had to wait on a flock of twenty or so geese to casually stroll across the road. When I finally arrived home Flora was standing in the garage smoking a cigarette. Flora was an occasional smoker. She normally only smoked when she was having a few cocktails. I hoped she hadn't started drinking already. I got out of my truck and approached her anxiously. As I got closer I noticed her eyes were swollen and bloodshot, not bright green. Her nose was red and there was no smile. This woman that I loved so much was almost unrecognizable.

I stood in front of her not knowing if I should hug her or just let her talk.

"I got a call from Raymond about an hour ago." Her voice quivered as she spoke, "He won't be picking up the kids this weekend."

I was disappointed, terribly disappointed, that we would not be able to make the mountains this weekend, but it seemed to be hitting Flora quite hard. I grabbed her and hugged her tightly.

"It's okay Sweetie" I said, "We can make the trip another time. Don't be so upset. We will still have fun this weekend."

I was relieved that that was the horrible news I had been dreading.

"That's not it" she said as she gently pushed me away. She was struggling not to cry.

"He doesn't want to see the kids this weekend because he just found out that he has terminal lung cancer. There's nothing they can do. He, according to the doctors, has maybe a year."

I was shocked. I had met Raymond on a few occasions. I would sometimes be at home before Flora on the days that he picked up the kids. He was a fairly quiet man, not overly friendly to me. Who could blame him? I was living with his ex-wife in a home he had bought with her and I saw his kids much more than he did. He was never rude to me, just didn't say much. However, without knowing him that well I knew he had to be a hell of a man. His children adored him and looked forward to their visits with him. They missed not seeing their daddy every day. And the fact that Flora had spent sixteen years with him let me know he had to be a great person. I felt awful for the kids and Flora too. She was taking it pretty hard.

"He feels that with him just now finding out that he would not be good company for Kyle and Taylor this weekend." Her voice was still quivering, "I just told them that their daddy wasn't feeling well and they would not be visiting him this time."

"I'm so sorry Honey" I didn't know what else to say. What could I say? How do you make a situation like this better?

Flora could not stop herself from crying any more. She broke down and started sobbing. I, again, grabbed her and squeezed her as tightly as I could. With her cheek resting against my shoulder she composed herself enough to say, "He wants me to tell them. He wants to appear strong for the kids and he knows that he will start crying if he has to look them in the face as he tells them."

"When are you going to tell them?"

"He wants me to tell them right away. He doesn't want to deceive them. He feels that they deserve to know what's going on."

We agreed that after dinner I would disappear for a while so that she could talk to them alone with no distractions. Both Kyle and Taylor love spaghetti, so I decided that would be dinner. I made sure I made things to each of their liking. Kyle preferred the garlic bread to be toasted on both sides, while Taylor liked it toasted on only one side. I usually did it one way each time we had it, and alternated from one side to both sides per occasion. But on this night I wanted both children to be satisfied. I made it both ways. There was only dark green lettuce in the salads—none of that almost white stuff. And I put on the kid's favorite music channel on TV as accompanying dinner music. I felt so badly for them I didn't know what else to do. Even though they didn't like me, I loved these children and I would have done anything to prevent the heartbreak and pain they were about to endure. I knew that after this night their feelings toward me would turn from dislike to hate. Their feelings of separation from their father would intensify knowing his time was short, and they would be seeing me every day walking around in perfect health. But all I had for them was love.

After dinner Flora and I cleared the table. The kids had been disappointed about not going to their daddy's house, but the smell of spaghetti had eased the pain somewhat. They both kept their faces in their plates throughout dinner only stopping to fill them up again....twice. Flora only nibbled. Once the dirty dishes had been put away I excused myself saying I had to run to the store.

"Will you get me a 'Yoo Hoo?" Kyle shouted from the living room.

"And some chocolate?" Taylor shouted.

"You bet."

I would get them anything they wanted and a thousand times more if I thought it would help them. I kissed Flora and told her I would be back in an hour or so. She was trembling.

"You need anything?" I asked her.

"No."

I gave her a hug and another kiss then walked out. The looks on the children's faces as they asked for treats was fresh on my mind as I drove to the store—innocent, trusting, and excited about their upcoming delights. I couldn't help but get watery eyed. I cried for them and for Flora. Not only were these little angels about to receive devastating news, Flora had to deliver it to the kids she loved dearly.

I arrived at the store and stayed in the truck for a while as I blew my nose and checked my face in the mirror. I didn't want anyone I ran into to know I had been crying—might ruin my macho image. I walked into the store and grabbed a cart. I wasn't getting that many things, it just felt better to have something to lean against as I walked. I picked up a three pound bag of Hershey's Kisses, a six pack of Yoo Hoo, and a dozen roses for Flora. I walked up and down the aisles taking my time. The drive back home was only ten minutes and I had been gone only twenty minutes. Normally when I spend this much time in a grocery store I end up with things I don't need like denture cleaner and pregnancy tests. If it's 'buy one get one free', I usually take advantage of it. But this time I didn't have food, toilet paper or batteries on my mind. I just wandered around pushing my cart, looking at people and wondering what was going on in their lives. Are they happy? Are they stressed? Are their lives complete? Does that big lady need all those 'Little Debbies'? I thought back to the time I first realized that I loved Flora. People seemed to be drawn to me as if I had the winning lottery numbers.

I was surrounded by positive energy and love. But on this particular night, the other patrons that I passed stared straight ahead. If eye contact was made, they would quickly look away. On this night I was still filled with love, but it came with heartache.

I arrived at home and found Flora and the kids sitting on the couch. The room was quiet, no TV. Flora sat in the center of the couch with Taylor to her left and Kyle to her right, each nestled under Mom's arm. The children didn't look up, and Flora gave me a look of despair with a forced a smile. I smiled back as I placed the Yoo Hoo, Kisses, and the flowers on the coffee table. Not wanting to disturb anyone further, I tip-toed upstairs to our bedroom and closed the door. I lay in bed staring at the ceiling for an hour or so and then fell asleep lying on top of the covers, in my clothes. At around 4:00 in the morning I awoke and found Flora lying in the bed next to me under the covers. I stripped down to my underwear, for comfort only, and slid under the covers next to her. Her back was to me so I moved next to her and put my arms around her. Flora quickly pulled away. I had apparently awoken her.

I had awoken Flora this way many times before as I was getting in to bed but she had never reacted this way, she had always moved herself closer to me. She turned and saw me.

"Oh Honey, I'm sorry." She said with sleepy breath.

She then nestled back next to me and we fell asleep.

The next day a dark cloud hung over the house. Everyone was still understandably in shock. It was Saturday and the kids stayed in their room all day only exiting for an occasional snack or drink. Flora was more mobile than the kids but she was also absent from me for the most part. I tried to stay out of everyone's way by running unnecessary errands, visiting with my folks, cleaning my truck inside and out, and arranging the pesticides on the garage shelf in alphabetical order. I went into the house at 5:15 to take a shower and then make dinner. I saw Flora sitting at the kitchen table. Her eyes were once again swollen from crying.

"You've been busy today." She said forcing a smile, as she patted the chair next to her asking me to sit down.

"Yeah" I said forcing a smile myself "Just trying to give you guys some space and stay out of the way."

I sat next to her and saw that she was still trembling and still struggling not to cry. I put my arm around her and kissed her gently on the lips.

"Honey" she said, "You know how much I love you."

"Yeah Sweetie, and I love you."

"Honey......."

She stopped as she still struggled to collect herself, "I have to do what's best for the kids right now. I love you so much. God, I love you...."

I sat in silence not knowing what was coming. After a few moments she was able to continue, "I'm asking Raymond to move back in with us. I'm sorry but you will have to move out."

"Huh?" was all I could say.

"I'm doing this so that the children can spend as much time with their father as they can in the time he has left, and so he doesn't spend his final days alone and without them."

"So why don't you just let the kids go live with him?" I asked selfishly.

"Honey, in the weakened state he eventually will be in, it would not be good for the kids and him to be alone. If he is here, he and the kids can be together and I can take care of all of them."

I was crushed. Last night I left so that Flora could deliver bad news to the kids, not knowing that they would be plotting the bad news to be given to me today. This isn't fair. What did I do wrong? Why do I have to leave? I couldn't believe that, once again, I was being thrown out the door by a woman that I loved. Hell, I tried my damndest not to love her, and now I'm regretting that night in Hilton Head. I didn't know what to say or how to react.

"Can we still see each other, talk, do things together?" I asked her.

Now I'm trembling.

"We can talk sometimes. But once he moves in we will live as a married couple. I must do this for the kids. They told me last night how unhappy they have been with our current situation. I had no idea. At this time especially they need their father." She answered, "I still love you Honey, but you are gonna have to move on and live your life as if I am married and unavailable."

Flora was starting to collect herself rather well now. My response to her statements probably helped her to realize what a selfish bastard I am.

"What about aft...." I caught myself and realized the insensitivity of the question I was about to ask. I felt horrible for what I almost said and horrible for my words and thoughts up to that point. I was about to ask if we could continue our happy fun-filled lives after her children's father dies. What a selfish bastard I am.

Flora knew what I was about to ask and sensed my regret.

She said so sweetly, "Don't feel bad Honey. I know what you meant. But I can't make any promises to you concerning that time until it arrives. I have no idea what the next few months hold for me or more importantly the kids."

Flora is about to be living with a dying man. A dying man she divorced, but loves. Two children are going to watch a father that they adore waste away in front of them.

A good man is going to die.

This is unfair to me?

What a selfish bastard.

~

Pyeville, GA is a small town located approximately 35 miles east of Atlanta and about 12 miles from Constance, where I had lived with Flora. It's an old town. By old, I mean that it has not grown very much over the past forty years or so—not a lot of new construction. Aside from the cars on the road, most sights in Pyeville could be used as the setting for a movie set in 1965. I think the residents liked it and planned it that way. It is rumored that during the Civil War, Sherman on his march through Georgia, bypassed Pyeville without burning it because he was acquainted with a few of its citizens. Because of this, it contains some of the oldest and most beautiful homes and business buildings in the state. The people of Pyeville love the look and the sense of history that exists here, and don't want it to change. From the tree-lined narrow streets, ancient street lights, 19th century architecture, store fronts, and even the aroma, you felt as though you had stepped back in time when you entered Pyeville.

Although the town's name did not originate from the dessert, at some time in the past someone decided that there should be some kind of correlation. Therefore, since 1953 Pyeville has hosted the state's largest pie cook-off. On the first weekend of every November the center of town is blocked off—no car traffic, and people come from all over the state and neighboring states to show off their pastries or to just fill up on them. There are blue ribbons awarded for best apple pie, pecan, pumpkin, blueberry, etc. There are also booths with people pushing their arts & crafts, candles, sculptures, quilts among other things. And the highlight of the event, which takes place on Sunday afternoon, is the pie eating contest. A large man from Prattville, Alabama has won the contest for four straight years—his large wife has come in second those same four years. The pie of choice for this event changes every year—last year it was rhubarb.

Pyeville is where I chose to live after leaving Flora's house. The main reason I chose it, it was the only affordable "Room for Rent" ad I found in the newspaper was located here. But it's also convenient because it's still close to work. I rent a room in a house owned by Louise Thornton. Louise rents out two of the three extra bedrooms in her old house to help with her own bills. The house is over a hundred years old. She also rents out her basement. The basement was totally redone and finished so as not to resemble the basement of a hundred year old house. She showed it to me when I first came to see the room as well as giving me details of the house's history and its age. I can't relay any of this information because I wasn't paying attention. The room that I rent is 12' x 12', consisting of a double bed, chest, TV, nightstand, and a closet designed for use in the 1800's. This particular closet can hold one 'Sunday go to meetin' suit, two pairs of overalls and a hat or two. A lot of my clothes were not hung, just stacked on the floor. Fortunately, the floor is carpeted. Unfortunately, it appears to have been carpeted in 1948.

Louise is divorced, probably fifty-five or so, and for the most part nice, but a little odd. She mumbles to herself—constantly. I think that maybe she has lived in this old house so long that some of the spirits of those that once lived here have entered her body, and they are having conversations with one another.

I once entered the kitchen to find Louise at the sink with her back turned to me—mumbling of course. She turned to see me standing behind her and the mumbling suddenly became audible and clear as if her monologue had been intended for me the whole time. It was scary, but I understood what she was telling me. Or was it one of the spirits? Louise and I get along well despite her oddities. I still try to avoid her. She always wants to talk, and I am never in any mood for idle conversation…or mumbling with her. She is odd.

Albert is one of the tenants. The room I rent is next to Albert's. Albert is retired. I have no idea what Albert is retired from, all I know is he smells funny. He is short, maybe 5' 5" tall and roughly a thousand pounds overweight. Okay, not really a thousand, but at least a hundred and fifty.

Albert, however, is very proud of his girth. I know this because he insists on walking around in nothing but his shorts. By shorts I don't mean underwear thank God, but short pants that have to be screaming from the abuse of being wrapped around this hippity-hop with legs. I can tell from Albert's grossly overhung gut that when he takes a piss he has no idea where it comes from. He also has some sort of nasal problem—a problem that obviously requires him to make loud, disgusting throat/nose sounds every fifteen minutes or so, always followed by a spit. I can hear this from my room at night. If Albert was a nice, friendly fellow I would maybe feel bad for the way I have described him. Albert's a prick. Like Louise, he mumbles, but not to himself. If you tell Albert "good morning", good luck deciphering his response. It's always said under his breath and never with a smile or even a look in your direction. The only time Albert talks clearly is when he is complaining about me being in the shower too long, someone eating his cheese in a can (yeah, it was me. Who can resist cheese in a can?), or anything else that sets this grumpy half-ton pile of cholesterol and mucus off. I don't like Albert. He smells.

The other tenant, Sue, lives in the basement. I don't see her that often because she has her own kitchen and bathroom down there. She works at a nearby pancake house as a waitress. The few times that I do run into her, I always try to spend a few minutes chatting. She's normal. During our chats I have learned a lot about her. Sue is widowed and without children, so her husband was really all she had when he died three years ago. It happened a week before their 37th wedding anniversary. She stayed in the house for five months after he died, but then had to move out and sell it because of the memories it held. They were happy memories, but a constant reminder that her beloved husband was no longer there with her. I really like Sue. She reminds me of an aunt of mine—sweet, never an unkind word, and always genuinely concerned with how things are going for me.

"How are you getting along, Sugar? I can tell by lookin' at you, that you aren't feelin' good" was a common greeting from Sue.

Even though she had no kids, she spoke to me in a motherly way. I always lied to her and told her I was fine. I didn't want to burden her with my problems. My problems were nothing compared to losing a companion of 37 years. I don't think she had to work but did so just to keep her body and mind both busy. Too bad she can't swap rooms with Albert. Sue is always fully clothed and smells like body lotion.

Needless to say, since most of my time at home is spent around Louise and Albert, I don't spend a lot of time there. That's how I found "Bernie's Bar and Grill". It's close to home—only a mile or so. It sits in the middle of town across from the square. On the other side of the square is "City Hall". "Bernie's" is part of a city block that has to be two hundred years old. The space it occupies is big—probably an old hardware or general store. Out in front, on each side of the door, is a bench. The two benches on the sidewalk were probably originally intended for people to sit on as they waited for a table, but they are now used to accommodate the smokers—no smoking inside. There was never anyone waiting on a table anyway. "Bernie's" was very often busy, but if there was no place to sit people would just nudge their way between occupied bar stools and order a drink as they stood and leaned against the bar. Since I smoke I spend a lot of time out front, usually standing. Through eaves dropping and an occasional conversation with a fellow smoker I have learned quite a bit about "Bernie's."

The place was opened twenty years ago and has been run ever since by Randy Fletcher. Randy's father, Bernie, had a restaurant by the same name in Charlotte, NC. Although the place in Charlotte was successful, Bernie had no intention of expanding. But when Randy moved to Georgia to attend the University of Georgia, he fell in love with and married a girl from Pyeville. Without remaining in school to get their degrees, they both dropped out midway through Randy's junior year. The two moved in with the girl's parents, and Randy got a job as a stock boy at the "Piggly Wiggly". Bernie Fletcher was not going to let his boy fail, even if he had to force success on him. He came down to Pyeville, found the spot to open the restaurant, bought it, equipped it, and was prepared to stay on a while to teach his son how to run a restaurant until he hit a snag—Pyeville was dry. This made acquiring a liquor permit difficult. You can't have a bar and grill without the bar. Bernie dropped the request for a liquor permit and opened the restaurant anyway. The huge bar in the middle of the restaurant served iced tea and soft drinks only, for the first year. Bernie did not give up, however. Knowing that it would be a challenge in a town that had more churches than fire hydrants, he set out to change the law in a city he had had no association with until a few months prior. It eventually came to a vote of the people of the city, but it was much easier than Bernie had anticipated. Apparently there were a lot of thirsty Baptists and Methodists in Pyeville needing a gin & tonic and a place to unwind away from the wife/husband and kids. Liquor sales passed with 59% in favor. The hard-core "Bible thumpers" were outraged and demanded a recount. They didn't get it. The mayor was thirsty too. "Bernie's Bar and Grill" was born. Bernie turned the keys over to Randy and headed back to Charlotte. Unfortunately Randy's marriage ended after five years, when his wife caught him giving one of his waitresses an unusually large tip after the bar had closed—a tip that required a shower afterward. Randy was upset for about two days until he realized that waitressing was usually a high turnover job, and that he would have the opportunity to tip many different waitresses in the future—Randy remains as owner and general manager—still un-remarried.

On one side of "Bernie's" is a jewelry store owned and operated by Charlie Kupp. Charlie's father had opened "Kupp's Fine Jewelry" over seventy years ago on the same spot it now stood. From what I had heard, Charlie was once a very sweet man, adored by everyone. He would always carry candy and/or quarters in his pocket to give to the children he would encounter throughout his day. He is a long time church deacon and obviously one of the 41% who voted against liquor nineteen years ago. Charlie is seventy-fiveish, short, a little stooped over (maybe that's why he's short), bald with bushy eyebrows & earbrows, and he is always holding an old wooden cane. But he absolutely detests the fact that hundreds of hell-bound, demon-possessed boozers inhabit the establishment next to the one his daddy founded. The jewelry store closes at 6:00 PM every day. But from the time "Bernie's" opens at noon up until Charlie closes his store, he steps out every so often to shoo away the smokers who step into the airspace in front of his façade. Charlie uses his cane to nudge them.

"I don't want my customers breathing in your foul smelling air and alcohol breath." he'll say, "Get back over to your side."

Most everyone knew Charlie and just did as they were told. Besides, who wanted to be the one to knock a feeble old man on his ass? Even though he was never pleasant to those who entered "Bernie's" I believe that they all still liked and respected Charlie. Most of the patrons grew up here in Pyeville, and probably remember him as the kind man who gave away candy and quarters.

On the other side of Bernie's is an insurance office. Hardly anyone ever entered or exited its door. The benches in front of it are also used by us smokers. No one seemed to care. Most of the parking is in the rear, with some parking along the street in front. There is an alley in the middle of the block for easy access from the back. At night, all cars on both sides belong to "Bernie's" clientele. It's the only place open past 6:00. Even though it is a ten minute walk from home, I drove. January nights can be kind of chilly. It's quite a risk because I usually leave hammered. Even though I sat alone and stared blankly at one of the TVs, the bar was becoming my home after work. As long as the taps on those kegs were operating, I was coming back.

~

Having Michael every other weekend was the only thing in life I had to look forward to. But because of my living situation and my small space at Louise's house, he stayed overnight at my parent's house while he was with me. Plus I was afraid that if he stayed there with me, Albert may get hungry and eat him. I believe he could have too. We were able to do things during the days that I had him, but at around 10:00 on Friday and Saturday evening I would leave him with my folks and return home. On my weekends without Michael, I would spend the better part of Saturday afternoon in the bar. The better part of the afternoon would then continue into the better part of the evening at the bar. But on one particular Saturday afternoon, after three months of solitary bingeing, I was approached by a man who I had seen many times before but had never met. I could see him approaching from my left out of the corner of my eye, just thinking he was passing by on his way to the bathroom. But as he got behind me I felt his hand on my left shoulder.

"Hey there buddy. How ya doin'?" He said.

I turned around and saw a balding man of about fifty looking at me grinning from hairline to hairline.

"I've seen you in here quite a bit so I thought I would come over and say hello. I'm Nathan." He continued.

I immediately knew that I was about to meet a used car salesman. I stuck out my right hand, and didn't have to force a smile. It actually felt good to be noticed by someone, even if it was a balding middle aged man. The smile was real.

"Hi Nathan, I'm Al. Nice to meet ya."

"Hey, I'm sitting over there with a couple of my buddies sharing a pitcher. You're welcome to come over and join us if ya wanna."

"Is there an open stool?" I asked.

"Yeah, right next to me."

"Okay."

I had exchanged words before with people sitting next to me at the bar, but nothing more than commenting on something we had seen while watching a game on TV, complaints about slow service, or an observation of low cleavage in the vicinity. Women had seen me alone and tried to talk to me, hoping for free drinks no doubt, but I would always find a polite way to let them know that I wasn't interested. I would tell them that I was gay, had herpes, was castrated in a bizarre Japanese hibachi bar accident, or I would say, "You're pretty enough, just too fat." or vice versa. I would let them down easy. I wanted only one woman, and I was still obsessed with returning to her. But Nathan had given me an invitation to do what guys do at bars— sit and drink beer by the pitcher while talking about nothing important and trade jabs with one another. I felt as though I had been asked to the big dance. The dance that involves conversing with multiple partners without having to watch your language, burping with no penalty for not saying "excuse me" (major penalties for farting, however), and escaping the reality that exists outside the doors.

Nathan put his hand on my back and said, "Come on over and I'll introduce you to the guys."

He led me to the front side of the bar where two other gentlemen sat.

"Hey fellas, this is Al"

That was followed by a "Hey Al" duet.

"Al, this is Sid and that's Bobby."

"What's up guys?"

Over the next three hours and seven pitchers I got to know Nathan, Bobby and Sid. Nathan IS a used car salesman. He is fifty-three years old, divorced, and dating one of the "Bernie's" bartenders, Stephanie. Nathan did have the personality of a used car salesman, but unlike a lot of salesmen, he appeared to be a genuinely friendly and outgoing person. I didn't need a used car and he didn't try to sell me one. It seemed as though Nathan was the one that linked this small group together. I can speculate that he had approached each of these guys, just as he had done with me, and united them in friendship. I knew, even in my drunken state, that I had a friend in Nathan as well.

Bobby is seventy-one years old, married and retired. He spends most evenings and obviously some Saturdays sitting at the bar. Bobby is fairly quiet, but as is the case with most people around his age, very interesting to talk to. His wife is in failing health, and he needs a couple of hours away from home to get away and have some joy in his life. He loves his wife dearly, he's been with her for forty-three years, but has to have time for himself each day. You never see Bobby in the bar past 8:30. He has to get home and help his wife to bed. Bobby is a baseball fanatic and very knowledgeable in baseball history. As a youngster, he was a batboy for the "Atlanta Crackers" minor league baseball team. He has had close encounters with many baseball hall of famers including Mickey Mantle and Hank Aaron. I, too, am a huge baseball fan, and as a kid studied its history and read anything & everything I could find on the subject. I knew that Bobby and I could spend days at a time talking baseball.

Sid is a total hoot. You always know when Sid is around because his voice and laugh can be heard from anywhere in the place including the bathroom. Sid is 50 ish. He is married and usually alone, but he sometimes brings his wife, Lori, with him to the bar. Sid works in the computer field. I don't know his exact profession, all I know is that he is fun to be around. He always has a fresh joke to tell and if you tell him you've heard it, he has another one you haven't heard. Even though Nathan appeared to be the leader of this group, Sid usually drew the most attention. I got up once and said that I had to leave for a while and Sid said, "Sit down. I'll get us another pitcher."

I am willing to be anyone's best friend if they buy me beer.

I was also introduced to a gentleman named Gino as he arrived to join the group. Gino was in the same general age group as Nathan and Sid. Gino is an electrician, separated with grown kids, lonely and bitter at the world. He mentioned his grandkids, he has three ranging in age from 2 to 6, and talked proudly and lovingly about them, including a stack of pictures he pulled out of his wallet. But as far as the rest of the world and life in general, Gino felt cheated. He was forced into a separation he did not want and blames all of his shortcomings in life on Communism....yes, Communism. Despite the "red scare" created by Gino I knew we had some things in common. I also felt cheated by life, but I tend to blame the "Protestants" more so than the Communists.

Over the next several days I entered "Bernie's" every evening to find at least one of these guys sitting at the bar. I now had someone to chat with instead of sitting alone and watching women's basketball. And there was often someone new sitting with the guys I had already met, so I was getting to meet more and more drunks to hang out with on every visit. I met Rod, a mechanic and a rabid NASCAR fan. Giblet, (That's his fucking name, not a nickname. His fucking name is Giblet. Pronounced: jib' lit) a young, twenty-something county water department employee who usually came in immediately after work in his county issued gray coveralls, covered all in brown stains, Lori, Sid's gorgeous wife, Jerry, a school bus driver who never arrived before six and was always gone by nine therefore making any parents present feel better about the safety of their kids, Jan, a cute little blonde receptionist with enormous melons and a tight bod, Paula, a not so cute music teacher, and Frank, an out of work actor (imagine that, an out of work actor in Pyeville, GA. Wonder why he's out of work?). I was not only meeting new people to sit with at the bar. Because of my new chummy situation with the regulars, the bartenders were now paying more attention to me and actually started calling me by my name instead of calling me "sweetie", "shoog", or "puddin". I also got to know them, the entire roster of "Bernie's" bar winches. Joanie, I've described before, Stephanie, a 40 ish slim brunette, also Nathan's girlfriend, Bonnie, a tiny blonde who had to stand on her toes to set a drink in front of you, Merilyn, who only worked a couple of days a week because of her kids, and Jenny, the sweetest and most beautiful one of all. Jenny is in her mid thirties, tall with light brown hair and big blue eyes. The bar always seemed to be full and for men only when Jenny worked, with additional vultures lurking around waiting for a bar stool to become available.

Visits to the bar had previously been a way to escape the hurt that I was feeling by consuming as much alcohol as was needed to numb the pain of losing Flora, often much more than was needed. But as I sat alone, I still thought of her. The visits had now become a way to escape my thoughts altogether, because I was now able to occupy my mind with conversation as I drank. But when I left, the hangover that followed was emotional as well as physical.

~

They say to stay away from religion when it comes to bar conversation. I don't know why, it's very interesting and also fun. On this particular Tuesday night I convinced all those around me that I am going to hell, and at the same time planted some doubts in their minds about their own beliefs.

Jan was sitting next to me, on my left. Jan is in her late thirties to early forties. She is very cute with short blonde hair, hazel eyes, and a smile that made her nose crinkle and her eyes sparkle. She is as sweet as she is cute. The first time we met, she hugged me and kissed me on the cheek. I felt pretty foolish standing there with my hand extended for a handshake. This was our first encounter after that meeting. I was sitting at the bar, and when Jan walked in she sat down next to me as if I was waiting there for her. I didn't mind, it was nice to have someone who looked and smelled pretty close to me. But I got the feeling that Jan was interested in more than just friendship. Under normal circumstances I would have been mutually interested. Along with her cuteness and sweetness she was sexy too. Jan's short—maybe 5', with a gorgeous tight body. If it weren't for her huge ta tas the bar stool she sat on would weigh more than she did. But fortunately for all men and lesbians present, she was anchored down well. She made it very difficult for me to remain faithful to my obsession with another, but I have to admit I enjoyed the attention she was giving me—rubbing my leg as she sipped her screwdriver.

On my right was Nathan. To his right was his girlfriend, Stephanie, who comes in to hang out at times when she's not working. Stephanie has a smoker's voice and a drinker's attitude. Behind the bar she is extremely efficient and professional, taking care of everyone she is responsible for without error. But on the other side, seated on a stool, she is just one of the guys. She gets loud, cusses, laughs and gets laughs. From what I have heard, Stephanie has dated many "Bernie's" customers in the past. It was Nathan's turn now. To Stephanie's right was Sid.

"Hey Merilyn!" Sid yelled to the bartender, "Why is this goddamn beer so warm? Is the fucking cooler working?"

Merilyn, a slightly overweight woman of around thirty, walked over toward Sid and said curtly, "You want a fresh beer, Sid?

"You're goddamn right I do. Put a few in the freezer if you have to."

Merylin did not work that often—usually one or two days a week. She was the substitute teacher that was called in when someone else couldn't work for whatever reason. Someone had to be there to take care of the over aged kids at the bar. She had been a full-time bartender at one time, but after having a couple of kids decided to spend more time at home with them. She was just as nice as the other bartenders, but I could tell that Sid was starting to push her buttons.

"Maybe you should drink faster so that it doesn't have time to get warm." She said.

"Me? Drink faster?" Sid laughed, "If I drank any goddamn faster I'd just order a keg and a straw."

"Do you have to take the Lord's name in vain so much?" Jan asked, obviously uncomfortable with Sid's language.

"It wasn't in vain." Sid said, "I got my point across. I got what I wanted."

"I don't like hearing it." Jan replied, "It sounds awful."

"Yeah, I don't like hearing it either." Merilyn said. She then glared at Sid and said, "Especially when it's aimed at me."

"Well" Sid said, "Ya'll just gonna have to put in some goddamn earplugs or kick me outa the place."

"If you say that word again," said Jan "I'll tell Lori that you were flirting with that slutty tattooed woman wearing the tight mini dress last Friday night."

"That's okay," said Sid "I was trying to pick her up for Lori. She likes her women slutty."

I looked at Jan and asked, "Why does it bother you so much? Just ignore it."

"I guess I shouldn't let it bother me so much," she said "cuz I'm not the one going to hell."

"Goddammit Jan, just lighten up," said Stephanie, "It's just a word."

"I like 'fuck' myself," Nathan chimed in, "not just saying it, but doing it."

"Too bad you're not as good at doing it as you are saying it." Stephanie quipped.

"Maybe if I had more practice at it, I would be."

"Go practice on your own."

Everyone laughed at Stephanie's comment.

"What do you mean?" I asked, looking at Jan, "What determines whether or not you go to hell?"

"Okay," she said, "Taking the Lord's name in vain doesn't automatically mean you're going to hell, but it doesn't hurt your chances."

"So what does determine where you will spend eternity?" I asked.

"Yeah, I'm interested in hearing this too, Expert." Nathan said, staring at Jan.

"Yeah," Said Sid, "enlighten us Saint Jan."

"If you don't believe that Jesus was the son of God, you're going to hell" she said, "It's that simple."

"So what determined it before Jesus?" I asked, "And when, exactly did the heaven and hell rules change?"

"After Jesus arose from the dead." said Merilyn, who had leaned against her side of the bar to join the conversation, "From that point on, you don't get into heaven without believing that Jesus was the son of God and that he arose after his crucifixion."

"That's the way I learned it," said Nathan, "But there sure are a buncha holes in that logic."

"Like?" Jan asked.

"Ya'll might as well forget it." Said Stephanie, "You ain't gonna change a Baptist's mind on this subject."

"I don't wanna change anyone's mind." I said. "But Nathan's right. Some of the things we were taught just don't make sense. And God forbid you should question any of it. 'That's what the Bible says, so that makes it true' was the only answer you would get. Well if you ask me, a lot of the Bible seems hard to believe."

"What do you mean?" Asked Merilyn.

"Okay," I said, "Merilyn said that after Jesus arose from the dead, you had to believe this to get into heaven—right?"

Everyone but Sid nodded. He had lost interest and was watching TV.

"Let's say," I continued, "that Jesus arose from the dead at 2:31 in the afternoon, Holy Daylight Saving Time. Exactly three minutes later, in what is now North Carolina, at 4:34 AM Cherokee Daylight Saving Time, a Native American woman died.

There is absolutely no way she could know about Jesus. As far as I know, smoke signals did not travel from the Middle East to North America. And even if they did, the smoke signals would probably be in Aramaic, not Cherokee. Does the woman go to hell?"

"That would be a judgment call by God." Nathan said, "He would probably let her in if she can cook a mean rabbit stew."

"No," said Jan, "Not unless she was hell-bound anyway."

"But how do you know?" asked Stephanie "It don't seem to be too clear."

I then said, "You're also saying that a Buddhist, a Muslim, a Jew, or any other non Christian who lives his or her life in a loving, caring manner, does no harm to anyone else, gives freely of their time and resources to help others will spend eternity in hell."

"Don't make sense," said Stephanie

"Here's another one." I said, "Adam and Eve were created by God—right?

Everyone nodded.

"If Adam and Eve were the only humans placed here on earth by God," I said, "that means that family members were having sex with brothers, sisters, Mom, and Dad in order to continue the human race. Where was the 'Garden of Eden'—Tennessee?"

"You're going to hell for sure after that statement." said Merilyn.

"No, Merilyn," I said, "I'm in hell and I am trying to climb my way out. Heaven and hell are states of mind, not physical sites."

I continued, "If anyone has an explanation for these things, I'm willing to listen. I'm open-minded. You can throw in that 'Noah's Ark' story too. How was he able to get two orangutans from Borneo, two penguins from Antarctica, two Boston Terriers from Boston, not to mention two of every single insect on earth—gotta be millions of 'em. I'm listening if you can explain."

"But that's what it says in the Bible." said Jan.

"Yeah, but who wrote the Bible?" I asked.

"Many people, not just one." she answered.

"People is right." I said, "People—humans—men and women wrote the Bible. It wasn't e-mailed or faxed from Heaven. It was written by people like you and me. Do you really believe that they were inspired to write what they wrote by a 'vision' or some 'Divine Guidance'? Maybe they were, but was it any more divine than the writings of Thomas Troward, Ralph Waldo Emerson, or Deepak Chopra?"

Everyone looked puzzled, wondering who these people I just mentioned were. I started to feel bad. I didn't set out to try and change anyone's beliefs. I just tend to get passionate at times when I am reminded of the pettiness and judgmental attitudes of certain religions. And the bullshit that is heaped on us to try and make the stories more interesting. Interesting stories are good, but don't try to tell me it's true when it obviously belongs in the "fiction" section of the library. I know that there are some historic facts in the Bible, but swallowed by a whale? Please.

"So what you are telling us, Al" Stephanie said "is that you do not believe in God."

"Yeah." said Merilyn, "You're telling us that if you can't see the proof it must not be true. If you can't see, hear, or touch God, he must not exist."

"You're both wrong." I said, "In my mind there is no doubt that God exists. All around us are sights and sounds of God. I believe that we were created. We didn't just magically appear. I just don't believe that the rules and restrictions put on individuals by some religions should make it so difficult for them to think and act for themselves. I don't need a book, a golden rule, or Ten Commandments to tell me what's right or wrong. I know not to covet my neighbor's ass—no matter how hot she is."

"So you believe in God, you're just not a Christian." Jan said.

"I'm not a Christian, but I believe everyone should try to be like Jesus, and Buddha, and Gandhi, and Mohammed. They understood life how we should live it. Yes, I celebrate Christmas, but there is no label on my belief because it's mine only."

"Hey Jan!" Sid yelled, "You happy? Nobody's said a cuss word for fifteen goddamn minutes."

"Fuck you, Sid" she answered

Everyone laughed.

"Fuckin' beer still hot, Merilyn." Sid complained further.

Merilyn went over to the ice bin and filled an oversized tin tumbler with ice. She then poured the ice into the blender and switched it on. She allowed the ice to rattle around getting crushed inside the blender for about twenty seconds as she grabbed a drink for someone on the opposite side of the bar. She returned, switched off the blender and poured the crushed ice back into the tumbler. Sid was pleased to see that Merilyn was making him a special coozie to set his beer in. Merilyn took the tumbler of crushed ice over to Sid, reached over the bar and dumped it in his lap.

"There." she said, "at least it'll be cold when you piss it out."

Sid knew he had it coming. He wiped the ice off of his stool and his pants. He sat and didn't complain any more about the beer's temperature.

"Thanks Merilyn." he said, "I would have dumped a beer in my lap, but you're obviously a lot nicer than me."

As everyone got a laugh out of Merilyn's daring move, Jan's hand slipped further up my thigh. I avoided the situation by saying that I had to go to the bathroom. I got up and headed around the bar to the other side, and down the hallway that led to the restrooms. How am I going to get out of this without hurting Jan? I have got to come up with a way without letting her know that I'm just not interested. I walked into the bathroom and to the sink. I stared into the mirror; light brown hair—medium length— neatly combed, clean shaven, blue eyes, five foot eleven, one hundred eighty pounds. On the outside I was a fairly handsome man. That's what Jan and the others saw. It's good that no one could see inside of me. Despite my previous declaration of belief in God, I recognized no Godliness inside myself. I was living in hell and full of hate. It was a hate that was aimed at no one or nothing in particular, but aimed mostly at the man staring back at me. I wanted to reach inside and grab him by the neck and choke him to put him out of his misery. Sitting at the bar was a cute sexy woman wanting to get to know me better, and all I could think about was how that might ruin my relationship with Flora—a relationship that may have already been ruined by my own selfish and uncaring behavior. I turned on the water and washed my hands, wishing I could wash away the pain I was feeling.

I walked out of the bathroom and toward my seat holding my cell phone to my ear. As I got closer to my friends I started talking to the imaginary person on the other end.

"Okay, I'll be there in fifteen minutes. Don't do anything until I get there."

As I got to my barstool, I didn't sit, but leaned against it and said to no one in particular,

"Problems at work. I gotta go in for a while." I then looked to Merilyn, "Can I have my check please, Merilyn?"

It was 8:15 PM. There are no problems at my job at 8:15PM, much less one that someone would call me for. But it was the best I could come up with, on the spot, to avoid Jan and possibly letting her down.

"Damn" said Nathan, "I didn't know you were that important."

"What are you," asked Sid, "a fuckin' CPO?"

"That's CEO, you moron" Stephanie answered.

"No" I said, "I just have to redo some orders that are going out early in the morning. Someone else did them wrong."

"You coming back?" Jan asked.

The look on her adorable face made me hate myself even more. Any other able-bodied heterosexual man would stay, have more drinks and then take her home. But I had tunnel-vision that saw me with only one other.

"No" I said as I patted her on the shoulder, "I'm gonna be there a while. I'll see you next time."

I put a twenty on the bar and walked out. I drove straight home, ate my dinner out of a can and went to bed.

~

Winter was not over yet, but on this particular Saturday morning in February it was 70 degrees outside. I drove to my parent's house to pick up Michael. We had planned a day at the zoo. I was excited and Michael loves the zoo. He spends hours at a time on the computer studying exotic animals and also drawing them, making homemade animations that are actually quite good. He really enjoyed the few opportunities he had to visit Flora at work. She would allow Michael to help her with the animals sometimes if the pet owner wasn't present. I pulled into the driveway, got out and walked toward the front door.

Out of the corner of my eye I noticed something moving to my right as I still stood outside the door. I ignored it, thinking it was a stray cat. But before I could turn the doorknob and enter, I got an icy cold blast of water on my back, drenching me from shoulders to butt. In shock and trying to catch my breath, I turned and saw Michael behind me, laughing hysterically, holding a giant soaker water gun. With the unusually warm weather, he was convinced that summer had arrived and it was time for outdoor water fun—the little shit.

"You little…"

Not able to finish what I wanted to say, I chased him around the house. He was giggling the whole time, while I was running out of breath chasing him. When I finally caught him, I beat him severely……not really. I wrestled the water gun away from him and then the chase reversed as I followed him, firing away. I allowed him to wrestle the gun from me after I stopped to refill it, and the saturation continued. By the time we got into the house we were both soaked, head to toe.

"Go get on some dry clothes," I told him. "we gotta get going."

Michael started for his room as my mother entered the kitchen where I stood.

"Where are ya'll off to tod…" she stopped as she noticed our wet clothes. "What in heaven's name happened to you two?"

"Instead of taking showers and getting dressed, we both got confused & got dressed and took showers."

My mother looked confused trying to make sense of what I had just said when I decided to help her out.

"Michael got out the giant water gun and used it on me then I used it on him."

She looked at me up and down with horror on her face.

"It's February and ya'll are behaving like it's July." She scolded "You need to put on some dry clothes. Let me get some of your daddy's clothes for you to put on."

I did not want to spend the day at the zoo wearing brown gabardine pants that stopped above my ankles and a white button—up short sleeve shirt with a pocket protector sewn in. I respectfully declined.

"I'll be fine Mama, my clothes will dry off on the way."

"On the way? You're leaving here wearing those wet clothes? Where ya goin'?"

"We're goin' to the zoo. We'll be in the truck for over an hour. I'll run the heater. I'll be dry when we get there."

"What about your underwear? It won't be dry. Let me get some of your daddy's for you to wear."

I certainly wasn't going to wear size 42" waist boxer shorts and have them bunching up on me all day. And I definitely was not going to tell my mother that it was no problem because I was not wearing underwear.

"I'll be fine Mama, don't worry."

"Well don't blame me when you come home with pneumonia."

"I won't Mama."

Michael came back into the kitchen wearing almost dry clothes. They were different but the pants still seemed to be wet around the seat.

"You did change clothes—right?" I asked him

"Yeah, Dad"

"Did you change your underwear too?"

"Oh yeah." he said as he raced back to his room.

When Michael had finally put on all dry clothing, (I should have made sure he changed his socks too, oh well), we jumped in the truck and headed for the zoo. This would be the first time that Michael and I would be visiting the zoo, just the two of us, without his mother. It had usually been a trip that was marred by constant complaints of tired feet, getting a headache, too hot, those monkeys' butts are gross, those pandas stink, haven't we already seen everything?, and that bathroom was nasty. But I took two Tylenols and promised myself that none of those things would bother me this time, for Michael's sake and enjoyment.

On the drive, we put the windows down to help my clothes dry. But while traveling at 75 mph with the windows down and wearing wet clothes, I was shivering. I put on the heater to warm myself up, just as I had told my mother I would do. Michael then complained that it was too warm. Maybe I shouldn't have made him change clothes, then we could both be comfortable. Anyway, I turned off the heater and froze during the drive.

"Hey Dad," Michael spoke up, "Why are there zoos? Shouldn't animals be left where they belong? Wouldn't they be happier?"

"If they were left where they belong," I asked through chattering teeth, "what would you and I be doing today?"

'Somethin' different I guess. I'm glad they have zoos. I was just wonderin"

I tried to make him feel better about the animals comfort.

"In zoos now, they try to make all the animals feel secure by making their surroundings a lot like their natural habitat. Not like when I was a kid. Most of the animals were just kept in cages then."

"What's habitat?"

"It's a certain animal's natural home. Remember that penguin movie?"

"Yeah"

"Okay, in that case, very cold temperatures, walking around on ice with an ocean nearby to find food and swim around in would be a penguin's habitat.

"Are there penguins at the zoo? I don't remember." He asked

"I think so. We're about to find out."

"How can the penguins' habitat be real? It's not that cold here."

"I think the penguins at the zoo are a different type. They don't need such cold temperatures."

I had no idea if that was true, but it sounded good and satisfied Michael.

We arrived at the zoo and drove around the parking lot

looking for an open space. A beautiful, warm Saturday in February obviously makes the zoo a popular place to visit. We finally found a space about a half mile from the front gate. It's not a long walk if you are a giraffe, but for a middle aged man in wet clothes and an eight-year-old, it's a hike. My mother was right. I was still cold despite leaving the truck and the blowing air inside. I did not, however, regret turning down my dad's clothes…….imagine the looks I would be getting. Instead I was getting strange looks because I was noticeably shivering on a warm day. We made it to the gate, bought tickets and went inside.

"Whata we gonna see first, Dad?" Michael asked with excitement.

"Let's just follow the trail and see what comes up first."

Flamingos, zebras, rhinos, elephants, giraffes, tigers, and crowds of screaming obnoxious human kids occupied the first thirty minutes inside. We followed the asphalt trail. Wooden signs with arrows beside the trail identified the attractions in each direction. We visited the reptile house. Michael loved looking at the snakes displayed in hundreds of separate glass terrariums, recessed into the walls, around a large museum type room. The glass between me and the snakes did not seem thick enough for me. I kept my distance, thinking one may burst through and sink it's fangs into my throat. After the snakes we saw the gorillas. The gorillas just sat quietly and stared at us as we stared at them. At the baboon and mandrill habitat, I averted my eyes as they paraded their bright fluorescent butts in front of me. We saw the smaller monkeys playing around and poking at each other as if they were playing tag. And of course, we saw the penguins. They seemed happy with the climate they were in—not too warm. I bought some popcorn and lemonade. Michael and I sat on a bench underneath a tree and enjoyed it.

"These animals have it made." I said to Michael, "Not a care in the world, they don't have to hunt for food—it's just given to them, they have a nice place to sleep, cover when it rains, and they're the star of the show. Wouldn't it be nice to be an animal?"

"We are animals, Dad."

"Oh yeah, I forgot."

We had seen almost all there was to see, when we came upon what would end up being the highlight of the day—maybe not the highlight, but certainly the most humorous part of the day for me.

"What are those two turtles doin', Dad?"

We were standing next to a short three foot high wooden picket fence. The fence had been set up in a large rectangle which covered about five thousand square feet—roughly the size of a basketball gymnasium. Inside the fenced area were ten or so giant tortoises scattered about. By giant, I mean four hundred pounds, at least. I was focused on one standing only a few feet from us when I turned to see where Michael was pointing. He was pointing at two turtles doing it....'tortoise style'. They were mating. I didn't really want to give a sex talk to my son here at the zoo. I turned to look at him and I could tell by his sly grin that he knew what they were doing, (kids learn a lot earlier these days). He just wanted to see what I would say. The male tortoise, (it was obvious) had his back feet on the ground and his front feet on the shell of the female. He did it very slowly, as we have learned that turtles do everything, but he would thrust inward every fifteen seconds or so, and each thrust would be accompanied with a deep, loud, throaty, "HUUUHHHHHHH"

I looked down at Michael and said, "They're playing leapfrog, and he's just having a hard time getting over."

We stopped for pizza on the way home. We arrived back at my parent's house at around 8:30. I was at last completely dry. I sat for a while and listened as Michael told them about his trip to the zoo. Thankfully, he omitted the tortoise story. We sat and watched TV until Michael's bedtime, 10:00. I kissed him goodnight and sent him to bed. As I was walking out the door my mom said to me, "We're going to church tomorrow. You want Michael to go with us?"

"What time you leaving?" I asked.

"Around 10:30"

"I'll be here at ten. If he wants to go, yeah that's fine."

I knew he would rather stay and watch cartoons in the morning, but I thought I would at least let my mother know that I was not stopping him from going to church. I then left to go home. I drove the entire way with a smile on my face even though I felt as though I was catching a cold. Could it have been the wet clothes? Was Mama right? I didn't care it was worth it.

I hadn't had very many lately, but this was a great day.

~

Gino and I sat at the bar, both of us mired in depression, and crying the blues over our pitiful lives. It was early in the evening, around 6:30, and none of the positive people were in yet, so we combined to create a depressing mood. Bonnie was tending bar and stayed away from the dark cloud that hovered over the two of us. She walked over occasionally to check on us but mostly stayed on the other end of the bar, probably afraid that the mood we had was contagious.

"I had to pay that bitch $750.00 yesterday to fix a roof on a house I don't even live in anymore." Gino said, "She'll probably be breakin' stuff on purpose just to get into my wallet, the connivin' bitch."

"If you don't live there anymore," I asked, "why do you have to pay it?"

"We're not divorced yet and the house is still in my name. I don't want it to fall apart. I need to get my money out of it if we sell it."

"Think ya'll might get back together?"

"Not likely."

"What about you?" he asked, "Think you and your ex'll get back together?"

I wanted to scream that I wanted that so badly, I would pour live fire ants down my pants if that would make it happen. But I didn't.

"Maybe. Too early to tell." I said calmly.

Gino focused his attention on two gentlemen on the other side of the bar.

"Look at those fucking queers." He said, "Makes me sick to look at 'em."

"Don't look at 'em, dumb ass."

Across from us sat two gentlemen, each wearing a shirt and tie. They were sitting next to each other, like Gino and me. They were drinking beer and talking, like Gino and me. They would look up at the TV and watch ESPN occasionally, like Gino and me.

"How do you know they're gay?" I asked him.

They're always in here together. They always sit alone and keep to themselves. I've heard things about 'em. Trust me they're queer."

He continued to stare at them.

"Looks like they're just having a beer and talking," I said, "just like you and me."

"They ain't nothing like you and me, unless you're a faggot."

I looked over at the men across the bar. One huge contrast between them and us was that they appeared to be having a pleasant conversation. They smiled and laughed occasionally. Gino and I had only been whining about the unfairness in the world, and how we were a couple of human bowling pins waiting to be knocked over again. As I continued to look at them I started to envy them, even if they were gay. Not that I want to be gay, I'm so heterosexual that I only watch 'girl on girl' porn. But I envied them because they appeared to be in a loving relationship.

Nathan walked in, came over, sat next to me and said, "What's up guys?"

"We were just talkin' about those fags over there." Gino said as he nodded across the bar.

"Wish they'd stop comin' in here." Nathan said, "Before you know it the place'll be full of 'em."

"You believe they're gay too?" I asked Nathan.

"Don't you?"

"I got no reason to. They're just sittin' over there drinkin' just like we are."

"Hey, don't compare us to them," Nathan said, "unless you're one of 'em. I haven't known you that long, maybe you are."

I took a huge gulp of beer, leaned back and said, "I am, Nathan. I've been waiting for a chance to be alone with you." I then put my hand on his knee.

Nathan looked at me in horror. I stared him in the eyes for about five seconds and then I couldn't stop from laughing.

"Fuck you." He said as he knocked my hand off of his knee.

"My point is," I said, "they're not bothering you. What do you have against them? Have you ever talked to them?"

"Hell no." said Gino, "They may think we're interested in 'em."

"Don't you ever talk to women that you are not interested in having sex with?" I asked, "What's the difference?"

"Actually," Nathan answered, "I don't ever talk to women I'm not interested in having sex with. But the list of women I wouldn't have sex with isn't that long."

"Yeah," said Gino, "He'd do his sister if it wasn't illegal."

"Illegal's got nothing to do with it." Nathan said, "My sister's married and my brother-in-law would kick my ass."

I then looked at Nathan in horror.

"I'm joking!" He said, "My sister's ugly anyway."

"Okay," I said, "If it was normal to be gay, could you force yourself to be gay?"

They both looked at me as if I had a cucumber growing out of my forehead.

"But it's not normal." Gino said.

"But if it were, could you force yourself to be gay?"

"Fuck no!" Nathan yelled, "I'm not giving it to no other man in the butt."

"I always pictured you as the one taking it the butt." Gino quipped.

"Pictured? How did that make you feel?" Nathan shot back

I was having fun. I enjoy making people feel uneasy sometimes. Homophobes are an easy target. I believe that some men feel that they have to be way over the top in their perceived disdain for homosexuals, just to make sure no one thinks that they are gay. I like Gino and Nathan, but it was amusing to make them so uncomfortable.

"I'm gonna go talk to them." I said.

They looked at me as if the cucumber was growing arms and legs.

"I'll bet that they're not even gay." I said, "I'll bet that they're just buds like we are."

"I don't wanna be that kinda bud." Gino said.

"You have a cute ass, Gino."

"Fuck you."

"I'm gonna prove that you two are letting those two, whom you have never met, ruin your goddamn day for no reason. I'm gonna go over and introduce myself and welcome them." I said.

"I guess this is goodbye." Nathan said, "You're going over to their side now. Nice knowing ya, Al. Stock up on the KY and Vaseline."

I gave Nathan a "fuck you", got up and headed over to the

other side of the bar. As I Turned to my right I noticed the "Neverlaid Brothers" sitting a few seats down from us having a conversation. Don and Phil must have overheard what Nathan had said. I heard Don yell out to Bonnie, the bartender, "Hey Bonnie, do you prefer Vaseline or KY jelly?"

Bonnie, who was pouring a drink, turned to see who her questioner was, and then refocused her attention on the bottle she was holding.

"I prefer Ky," she said, "but you two needle dicks could probably get by without either."

I had had a few beers and decided to make a trip to the bathroom before approaching the alleged "fairies". As I washed my hands, I checked myself in the mirror. I then scared myself because I was making sure that my appearance was presentable before approaching two men who may be gay. Hell, why not? I would, of course, turn down any proposals, but a proposal would still be flattering.... wouldn't it? Is handsome, to gay men, the same as handsome to women? I decided to end this confusing debate with myself and exited the men's room. I walked up behind the two "Nancy Boys" and tapped each on the shoulder as I stood, centered behind them. They turned and saw me. The one on my right appeared to be in his mid thirties and the other appeared a little older.

"Hey guys, I'm Al. Haven't seen you in here before. This your first visit?"

I flashed back to the day Nathan first introduced himself to me (I wonder if he had bets on whether or not I was gay). But this time I was the regular welcoming someone I didn't know.

"No, Al. We've been in before, just not in a while." said the older one, "I'm Robert, and this is my partner, Joe." as he nodded to the other.

They both extended their hands. Those two hillbillies across the bar were right. They are gay. I was now starting to feel uncomfortable.

"Haven't been here in a while?" I asked, "What's been keeping you away?"

"Been too busy at work." Joe said, "Lawyers don't have a down season. That can be a good thing, but not when you need a vacation."

"Yeah," said Robert, "but since we merged and became partners, at least someone can always be there to handle the load."

Joe then added, "We would come in here every night to unwind but it's gonna be tough enough just to come up with an excuse for our wives on why we're late tonight."

Partners in a law firm....wives... Forget what I said about the hillbillies across the bar.

"Look forward to seeing you again." I said, "Nice meeting you both."

I patted them both on the back and started to walk away. But I couldn't resist. I turned and walked back over to them.

"Hey Robert, Joseph"

They turned back around. I pointed to Gino and Nathan across the bar.

"Those are two of my friends over there."

Gino and Nathan saw me pointing their way and both looked at me nervously. The overhead music was loud enough so that they couldn't hear me.

I continued, "That's Gino on the left and Nathan on the right....wave to 'em."

Robert and Joseph obliged. Nathan and Gino raised their hands and forced a smile.

"They're good guys. Say hello to 'em next time you're in."

"Will do, Al." Joseph said

I did resist the urge to ask them to blow a kiss their way. I said goodbye again and headed back to my side of the bar. Both Gino and Nathan were glaring at me as I sat down.

"You guys were right," I said, "their partners."

"Knew it." Said Nathan

"I didn't need no proof." Gino said arrogantly

"They're partners in a law firm." I said, "They have to get home soon so their wives won't get pissed, you two homomorons."

I continued, "I'm sorry to disappoint you, but ya'll are just gonna have to find someone else to hate."

I looked around the bar to see who was there. I noticed a man wearing a green shirt at the end of the bar, opposite of where we were sitting. He had medium length brown hair and a neatly trimmed goatee. He was sitting next to a very attractive, busty blonde.

"Look at the guy down there in the green shirt." I said

They both looked at the man.

"I bet he's a Communist. No, I'm sure of it. Look at 'im. Yeah, he's definitely a pinko commie." I rubbed it in.

"Still think they're queer." Gino mumbled.

"You're disappointed aren't cha?" I asked, "You were happier when you were able to look down your nose at those two because you thought they were gay."

"Hey," Gino said, "that's just my opinion."

"Look at that woman with the commie." Nathan said.

"Yeah," I said, "I noticed her. Isn't it better to look at her and fantasize than to sweat two supposedly gay guys?"

"I'm glad Stephanie's not working." said Nathan, "If she was here and saw me staring at her I'd get cut off…and I don't mean beer."

Gino then asked, "Why the fuck are ya'll even interested in a girl that is obviously involved with a Communist?"

"Gino, he's not really a Com…" I stopped. I didn't want to go into another hate fest.

We were having fun. The jabs and ribs were good-natured and we were not afraid to throw them around. No one was ever really upset with another. That's how men bond. By the time we left, we were all usually loaded enough to give each other a hug. Not too tight though—we're not gay for Christ's sake.

~

I woke up one morning to find a note had been slipped underneath the door to my bedroom.

"Al, I would appreciate it if you would be quieter at night when you come home. I have to get up early for work and have a tough time falling back asleep when I am awakened. Also, would you please park in the street from now on? You're truck being in the driveway makes it hard for me to maneuver my car in and out of the garage. I would appreciate your cooperation and expect you to comply with my requests. Louise"

She has got to be kidding. I tip-toe up the stairs, open and close the door slowly, even holding the knob so you can't hear a click when it closes. When I watch TV, I have the volume so low, only I can hear it. I've made sure of this by standing in the hallway with the door closed, and the TV on, to be sure. On the previous night, I had arrived home at 8:30. Who needs to be super quiet, anyway, at 8:30? It's not my fault that the old house creeks and pops with every little movement. It's absolutely impossible to make zero noise in a hundred plus year old house. I was pissed! The old lady must have been feeling unimportant and needed to make a statement to let me know she's boss. I stormed out of my room. I ran back to my room and put on my robe when I realized I was in my underwear. I was anxious to unload on the psycho bitch. I ran downstairs looking for her, but she was not around. I guess it's a good thing she had already left for work, otherwise I would probably be needing a new place to stay by the end of the day. Confronting her in my present state of mind would not have been pleasant. But I wasn't ready to cool off yet.

As I had mentioned before, Louise is pretty odd. Up until this point she had been friendly toward me, but I had noticed instances of her acting mentally unstable. I once had heard her yelling at Albert, while I was in my room, "I just bought those chips! Why did you have to eat every fucking one of them?"

I actually felt sorry for Albert after hearing this. He probably had no idea he had done anything wrong. It is his job to eat, and if he doesn't have to hunt for it, all the better. I think Louise set him up by leaving the chips on the counter. She needed someone to yell at and knew Albert would not be able to resist emptying the bag.

Another time, as I was walking through the kitchen, Louise was going through her mail. She opened up an envelope, looked at its contents and yelled, "Goddamn assholes!"

Apparently the cable bill was not to Louise's liking. She then got on the phone with the cable company and proceeded to unload a tirade of obscenities that I could hear, even though I had entered my room and closed the door by this time. Her language made me blush. But now that her venom was aimed at me, I was determined not to lie down and give in to her. The day I first came to look at the place, before moving in, she was Mary Poppins. But on this day she had morphed into Cruella de Vil. Albert was always a dick. Sue was always sweet and friendly. Louise was a coin flip, you had to be careful.

After noticing that Louise had left, I turned my attention

toward breakfast. I was still fuming over the note as I rummaged through the cabinet for some pop tarts I had left in there....gone, of course. My food is safer in my room, although even then, Albert could probably sniff it out and pounce on it. As I was about to close the cabinet I noticed four cans of tuna on the shelf. I knew that they belonged to Louise. She had mentioned her diet to me one day while I was trying to ignore her, and it involved eating a lot of tuna. An evil thought popped into my head. I pulled the tuna out of the cabinet and set them on the counter. I walked to the bottom of the stairs and peeked upstairs to make sure that Albert's door was still closed. I didn't want any witnesses to what I was about to do. I walked outside and entered the detached garage behind the house. On a shelf in the garage Louise kept several cans of cat food. There was a stray cat that hung around the house and Louise always set out a dish of food for it so that it wouldn't starve. That was the kind side of Louise. I was out for revenge toward the nasty side of her. The shelf contained various flavors of food. I pulled down four cans with flavors that most closely resembled tuna—ocean whitefish, tuna, salmon, and cod. The cat food cans and the tuna cans, I had set on the counter, were exactly the same shape and size—how convenient. I took the cat food inside to the kitchen. I took another peek upstairs at Albert's door. I don't know why I was so concerned with being seen by Albert without my knowing. He can't sneak up on anyone. He shakes the rafters with every step. I carefully peeled the labels off of the cat food cans and set them aside. I did the same with the tuna. I was surprised by how easily they came off. I then switched the labels—cat food labels on tuna, tuna labels on cat food. I secured all the labels with a dab of super glue. I placed the faux tuna in the cabinet and took the tuna dressed in cat food clothing out to the garage. The stray cat was sure to be pleased by my prank—real food.

Feeling good about myself and not as mad at Louise anymore, I went back upstairs to get ready for work. Knowing that she would soon be scarfing down "Nine Lives" had cooled my anger somewhat. I showered, got dressed, and headed outside.

Before getting into my truck, I stepped back to get a better view of the space between my truck and the garage. It was a straight shot into the garage, passing by my truck parked to the side and in front of the garage. There was six feet of space between my truck and garage entrance. Her other request, that I park in the street, was obviously just another way to spew venom my way. I decided I would wait for my revenge on this matter. Spring was starting to arrive, so I knew that freezing temperatures were probably gone until next December. But if I am still living here next winter, on the night of the first hard freeze, I will pull out the water hose in the middle of the night, and soak down the entire driveway. Margaret will be unable to leave the house because of the slight upward grade from the garage toward the street. Her attempt to leave may possibly cause her to slide backwards uncontrollably and into the side of the house. I, on the other hand, will be able to leave and arrive safely being parked in the street. Albert doesn't drive and Sue parks in the rear beside the basement door. I can't wait for winter to arrive.

I got into my truck and left for work. I knew that my devilish prank would make me a few minutes late, but I felt as though it was worth it. On my drive my thoughts started to drift toward Flora, as they most often do. It had been three weeks and two days since I had last had any contact with her. She had sent me a smiley face after I had sent her an "I miss u" text. I wondered if she thought about me as often as I thought about her. Are her thoughts about me happy thoughts? Is our time apart causing her to miss me, or realize she is much better off without me? I wondered if she sniffed the few items of clothing I had left behind to remember my scent. Does she lie in bed and imagine my hands gently caressing her body? I wanted her to be happy, but the egotistic part of me wanted her to be miserable because of my absence. We were together for a short time, as far as romantic relationships go. But things were so perfect for us in that time, that I knew I could never be as happy with anyone else as I had been with her.

When I first moved out of Flora's house, she and I kept in touch by speaking at least once a day by phone. The conversations were usually short because the only time we could talk was when she was at work. She did not want to talk to me around Raymond and the kids. That would create an awkward situation for all involved. I understood that, but being the selfish bastard that I am, I would often become emotional during our talks because of the loneliness and frustration I was feeling by not being able to see her. I said some things that I did not mean out of self pity. I blamed her for my isolation and misery. Shortly after these talks I would realize that I had been unreasonable and was being a selfish bastard. Unfortunately I could not see that I was being a selfish bastard at the moment that I was being a selfish bastard. She was going through a horribly tough time herself witnessing a life as it slipped away, and with her children who did not deserve this type of devastation. I, on the other hand, was hanging out at a bar every night getting drunk.

I was putting her through additional hell with my constant cries for attention and laying my sadness on her. She did not deserve this. As kind and gentle as Flora is, I kept pushing her further and further away. Finally, she had had enough and said that we should not talk anymore. I respected her request somewhat. I did not call her every day, but I would still text a couple of times a week just to tell her I missed her and loved her. Sweet Flora, even though she had asked me to leave her alone, would answer each text with a smiley face. I knew that she still loved me, but I was so goddamned self-absorbed that I could not accept being less important to her than anyone else. I eventually stopped sending the texts and left her alone. After four months apart, I stopped contacting her completely hoping she would reach out to me eventually. I realized, possibly too late, that my contacts with her were only hurting my relationship with her. As morbid as it may seem, I held out hope that we would be together again after Raymond died.

I arrived at work fourteen minutes late. I assumed my spot at the counter behind the computer screen. My immediate boss had not noticed I was late because he was upstairs in a meeting. My job requires me to take and fill orders of various construction items for building contractors, subcontractors, handy men, and such. It is not a very stressful job unless you run out of a specific item that is required immediately by "Bob the Builder". It is usually my fault when that happens, of course, and I have to stand there and accept responsibility (I can't actually tell Bob that it is not my job to order the material. That job belongs to my boss). But those situations are most often remedied by offering a discount on another item or promising free delivery of item as soon as it arrives. My highest stress level, however, is achieved when dealing with "Barb the Builder". Don't get me wrong, I am not a sexist or one to insist that men are more capable at certain professions than women. But the female contractor knows more than any man alive. There is nothing worse than dealing with a paranoid woman who believes that every man is out to take advantage of her thinking: Isn't it cute? She can use a drill.

A semi attractive brunette with her hair in a pony-tail, wearing blue jeans, a loose red t-shirt, and brown construction boots approached me at the counter.

"Good morning" I said to her.

"Hey. I need forty of them one by six spruce fence boards, six foot dog-eared." She said assertively.

"I'm sorry Maam, we only carry those in cedar and treated pine."

"No. Ya'll got 'em in spruce. I got 'em here before, many times." She answered in her nasal twang.

I had worked here behind this desk for over seven years. I do not recall ever seeing this woman. Perhaps she was lost. Perhaps her other visits had been during times I was not working. Perhaps she did belong in another profession.

"No Maam. We only have the cedar and treated pine. I'm sorry." I said in a sympathetic tone.

That was a mistake. The sympathetic tone told her that I was talking down to her. Her eyes got red, her face turned red, and I swear to God, her hair turned red. She raised her right hand above her head. I thought she was about to take a swing at me, but instead she slammed her fist down on the counter.

"I am not stupid! I know what I am talking about!!! I need forty spruce boards and I need them today!!! You have them, just tell that fat piece of shit in the back to get them for me, you smart ass fuck!!!!"

I didn't bother to wipe her spit off my face in front of her, fearing that she may take it as an additional insult. I could not fill her order as she wanted because we didn't have what she was requesting. I had to think of something quick because everyone in the store was now looking straight at me, wondering how I was going to respond. I remained calm. I had always been taught to never hit a lady.

"Yes Maam. Why don't you come with me to the supply area and we will find them?"

I came from around the counter to where she was standing. I kept my distance, however, not knowing if she was ready to hit me. I motioned my hand to the back of the store.

"Follow me and we will find the spruce boards." I said.

"Why can't you just get 'em for me, asshole?" She sweetly queried.

"Since I am not familiar with the spruce boards, I need you to point them out for me." I reasoned.

She let out a sigh of disgust, rolled her eyes, snatched up her purse and stomped behind me. I had no idea what was about to happen, but at least I was getting her away from the other customers. I walked her to the back, through the swinging double doors that lead into the lumber yard and headed toward the fence material. All the material was stacked on pallets and labeled.

"There they are." She said pointing to a pallet of boards. "I knew you had 'em, dumbass."

She was pointing to a stack of boards clearly labeled with a cardboard sign; "TREATED PINE". She either couldn't read or was too obstinate to admit her mistake. She did, however, know all cuss words even if she couldn't spell them. Although I had been referred to as "smart ass fuck", "asshole", and "dumb ass", by this woman, I decided to take the high road since it was my job to be nice and she may have been illiterate.

"Sorry Maam….my mistake."

I instructed the yard man, Claude (the fat piece of shit she had referred to), to gather up forty of the boards for the nice lady. I hope she doesn't get a nail in her tire as she pulls around to load them.

For the rest of the day there was no direction to go but up. It was odd that a day could start with so much negative estrogen flowing my way. As the day wore on the anger I had felt started to dissipate. I actually started to feel bad about the tuna hoax I had pulled on Louise—not enough to go back and reverse it, but maybe I will forget about the icy driveway episode next winter. That is unless she manages to piss me off again.

~

I walked into "Bernie's" at around 7:45. It was a Thursday and the bar was unusually packed for this time on a weeknight. Even though the bar itself was full, the tables and booths were nearly empty. Only a few people were seated and having dinner. I saw Nathan and Gino seated at the bar, on the opposite end of our normal spot—toward the back of the room. As I walked toward them I could see why the bar was full. Jenny was bartending and wearing the tightest t—shirt I had ever seen on a woman. There was no room even for a wrinkle and Jenny filled it out very well. She knew how to bring in the tips. I then noticed that almost everyone seated at the bar was male. I walked up behind my buddies and said "hello". They both turned around.

"She's puttin' on a helluva show tonight." Nathan said. "Look, her t-shirt doesn't reach her jeans and every time she bends down she shows butt cleavage."

"That's nice." I said, "It would be nicer if I had a place to sit so I could enjoy it."

"Hey, Jenny!" Nathan yelled, "Can we get another cold mug over here?"

Jenny, who was leaning into the beer cooler arose and looked toward Nathan to see me standing behind him. She opened the beers she had emerged with, sat them in front of two gentlemen sitting to our right, pulled a beer mug from the freezer and walked over our way.

"Hi Al." she said as she sat the mug on the bar, "A lot of people are paying their tabs now. A stool will be open soon."

"Thanks Jenny. Bring us a pitcher on me please."

"You got it sweetie."

Nathan and Gino were already at the bottom of their pitcher, and from the looks of Gino, it wasn't their first. Although I had been standing there behind them where they sat for a few minutes, he had not uttered a word. He didn't even tell me "hello" as I first arrived. He was focused straight ahead looking at nothing in particular. I got Nathan's attention and as pivoted on his stool to look at me I nodded toward Gino.

"What's with him?" I asked in a hushed voice.

"You hear what happened today?" Nathan asked me.

"No. What?"

"Charlie Kupp died."

"What happened?" I asked.

"At lunchtime today, he walked out of the door of his store, probably to give all the smokers hell, and he dropped dead. They say he grabbed his chest, took a couple of steps, tried to lean on his cane, and just fell forward onto the sidewalk—apparently had a heart attack." Nathan then motioned toward Gino with his beer mug and said, "I haven't seen him this depressed since Buck Owens died."

"He made 'Hee Haw' what it was." Gino said.

"Yeah, he did." Nathan sarcastically agreed.

"He was my Sunday school teacher from the time I was eight till I was twelve." Gino spoke about Charlie, "He was a good man.

He wasn't the grumpy old cuss everybody thought he was. He was a nice man."

I gave Gino a sympathetic pat on the back. Since I had no place to sit anyway, I headed outside to have a smoke. I had only seen Charlie on a few occasions, and never talked to him or got to know him. But it is always a shock when someone you even vaguely know dies. I walked out the door and lit up a cigarette. There were a few others outside with me. Rod and Frank were sitting on one of the benches.

"You here 'bout Charlie, Al?" Rod asked me.

"Yeah, just found out. I'm sorry to hear it."

Rod, a mechanic, and Frank, an out of work actor, both had grown up in Pyeville and knew Charlie well.

"He was a sweet old man. Couldn't tell it from the way he acted around here, but he was always nice to me. Gave me bubble gum all the time when I was a kid." Rod said.

Frank then spoke up, "He put up the money one time to stage a play here at the park every Friday night. Bought the wardrobe, the props, furnished the chairs and even helped build the stage. We'd do Shakespeare right there in the park. Charlie said it was needed to add a little culture to the community—didn't last long, only a couple o' months. Not many people showed up and we weren't getting paid enough to act in it. Charlie lost everything he had put into it but he didn't seem to mind—just said that Pyeville obviously wasn't ready for any culture."

"Shakespeare…. Here?" I asked.

"Yeah, that's the same attitude most everybody else around here had." Frank answered.

I looked over to Charlie's store. Nothing looked different. It was always closed at this time of day anyway. There was a young man and a young woman standing close to Charlie's door smoking. I looked down at the imaginary line on the sidewalk that separated his property and the bar's. I knew that inconsiderate jerks would now be crossing that line with their cigarettes in hand, and suffer no repercussions. I was mad at this couple and they surely had no idea that they were doing anything so reprehensible. Charlie's spirit may have been near and causing me to feel this anger.

I wanted to do something for Charlie. I never met him, but everyone who knew him talked about him as if he was Jesus Christ (Didn't Jesus get mad and bust up a place once? It wasn't because of smokers, I don't think). People honor Jesus every day—people who have never met him, only read and heard of him. Well, I thought I should find a way to honor Charlie on this night. He didn't perform miracles, as far as I know, but he positively touched the lives of everyone who knew him. I never met him—only heard great things about him. I put out my cigarette and went back inside.

A stool had opened up next to Nathan so I sat down and took a sip of beer. I knew we had to do something, just wasn't sure what yet.

"We need to do something for Charlie." I said to Nathan.

"He's dead. Not much we can do for him now unless you've built a time machine you haven't told me about."

"I mean in his honor, numb nuts."

"Oh. Whadja have in mind?"

"Don't know."

"I drove by earlier today and the police were there." Nathan said. "Had the whole front of the store taped off out to the street so no one could get near it—shoulda seen it."

"Sounds like a murder scene."

"Looked like one."

A thought then popped into my head. I wasn't sure how we would do it yet, but I had an idea. It wasn't a brilliant idea, kind of crude, but a way to honor, and I'm sure please Charlie.

"Where can we find some orange construction cones?" I asked Nathan.

Nathan put his thumb and index finger on his chin and thought for a couple of seconds.

"Yeah." He said, "Their redoing the sidewalk down on Pearl street—got 'em lined up all along the edge of the road. Why?"

"Let's go." I said as I arose from my barstool.

"Go? Go where?"

"Gino, we'll be back in a few minutes." I said, "You're in charge of the beer til we get back."

Gino was loaded and didn't seem to mind that we were leaving. I'm sure he was happy to watch the beer for us and act as collateral for our bar tabs.

"K" he said.

Nathan, on the other hand, was confused.

"Whata you up to? Why we leavin'?" he asked with a worried look

"Come on" I said as I was walking toward the door.

Pearl Street was only a couple of blocks from the bar. Nathan jumped in my truck and I filled him in on my plan as I drove. There were no cars parked on the street as we arrived, all the businesses were now closed for the day. We drove along until we arrived at a spot where the sidewalk had been crumbled up and removed. I stopped the truck next to the curb. Orange cones lined the street for about two hundred feet, spaced approximately three feet apart to keep pedestrians away from the mess and workers. I suddenly realized that if we wanted these cones, they had to be stolen. I got nervous. We only needed about eight of them, and there were so many I hoped that as long as we weren't spotted during the act, they wouldn't be missed. It was dark out, but the street lights made it difficult to not be seen by a passing car. We got out of my truck and stood at the edge of the good sidewalk for about three minutes discussing our plan. We wanted to get an idea of how busy the street was at this time of night. Only one car passed.

"Okay," I said, "We need eight cones. We'll walk down together and get two each, return to the truck, and then return for two each again."

"Quit makin' it sound like we're planning a fuckin' Brink's heist. They're orange cones." He said.

"Stealin' is stealin' and I don't want to go to jail." I said, "Don't take two right next to each other. I don't want it to be noticeable that any are missing."

"Let's just get 'em." He was already walking away.

I followed. We each grabbed two cones and brought them back to the truck. I stacked them on top of each other and laid them in the bed of my truck. We headed back to pilfer the rest. We each grabbed two more and as we walked back with them, we noticed headlights coming down the street. We got to the truck, sat them on the sidewalk next to the truck so they couldn't be seen by anyone in the car, and waited for it to pass. But the car did not pass. It stopped next to my truck, "Pyeville Police Dept." stamped on the door…. I'm going to jail. Orange construction cone theft is going to be on my record. The ironic thing is: I will be wearing an orange jumpsuit, surrounded by orange construction cones as I pick up trash on the side of the highway.

"What you boys up to?" There were two officers in the car. The one on the passenger side spoke with his window down, still sitting in the car.

"We were looking at this vacant space." Nathan spoke up.

If this officer gets out of the car, he will be able to look into the bed of my truck and see the cones we have already placed in there. I'm going to end the night with ink on my fingers.

Nathan continued, "My girlfriend is looking for a spot to open up a nail place. A buddy of mine told me about this site and we just wanted to ride out and look at it"

I turned around and saw a 'For Rent' sign in the window. Good eye, Nathan!

"A nail place?" The officer responded with a puzzled look.

"You know? Where women get the manicures and pedicures." Nathan said.

"Oh yeah." The officer said, "My wife spends a quarter of my salary in those places—tried to get me to go, but I can't take the chance of one of my buddies walkin' by and seein' me gettin' my toenails polished."

We both laughed. I was starting to feel a little easier.

The policeman continued, "Come back and look at it in the daylight. It's a nice spot."

"Will do." Said Nathan, "Thanks a lot."

"Good luck with it. You boys have a nice evening." The cops then drove away.

"Good job bro." I said to Nathan

"Not the first time I had to lie my way out of a jam. Don't tell Stephanie how good I am at it. I'll never get away with nothin'."

We stacked the cones and put them in the truck. I then drove to the Wal-Mart about two miles out of town. Nathan waited in the truck to guard the cones while I ran inside. I don't know why he wanted to guard the cones, but I let him. After ten minutes I returned to the truck, threw my bag into the bed and we went back to the bar.

I drove right up to the front door and let Nathan out at the curb. He got out, grabbed both stacks of cones and stood them on the sidewalk. I left to park the truck. I returned to the front door, holding the bag I had gotten at Wal-Mart, and found Nathan still outside waiting for me.

"You ready?" he said.

"Let's go in and have a beer first."

As we got to our spot at the bar, I noticed that Gino had already finished the pitcher I had bought and had apparently ordered another. A full pitcher sat in front of him. He turned to see that the two of us had returned.

"I put this pitcher on you, Nathan. It was you're turn."

"That's fine, Gino."

"Where the hell ya'll been?"

"Stealin' stuff." I answered.

"Get anything good?"

"Orange construction cones."

"Never seen any of those in a pawn shop. Can you get much for 'em?"

I gave Gino a friendly look, patted him on the back and said, "We're gonna use 'em not sell 'em."

I yelled Jenny's way, "Can we get two more cold mugs here, Jen?"

Jenny leaned over into the freezer to get two mugs as we all drooled over her. She walked over and sat them in front of us.

"Thought you two left." She said, "I was pissed, cuz you didn't say goodbye."

"Unpiss yourself," I said, "we're back. I'll give you tongue before we leave."

"Promises promises."

I poured beer into my mug and then chugged it down without stopping to take a breath. I grabbed my bag and headed outside.

"You comin'?" I asked Nathan.

"Give me chance to drink my beer, Speedy."

I went outside, unstacked the cones and started lining them up. A few folks were standing outside watching and wondering what the hell I was doing. Two men were standing in front of Charlie's store smoking. I looked at them and asked, "You two mind standing somewhere else? I'm doin' somethin' here."

They both looked annoyed but obliged and moved back to the front of "Bernie's". I placed two cones, side by side on the sidewalk from "Bernie's" storefront to the street at the edge of Charlie's store. I then lined up four cones, placed three feet apart at the edge of the street along the front of Charlie's store. I then placed two more cones at the opposite edge of Charlie's store from the street to the storefront. I then opened up my bag and went around to each cone placing a 24" wooden stake into the top of the cone. At the top of each stake was a 6" x 10" plastic sign that read, "NO SMOKING" in bright orange letters on a black background. Nathan and Gino both came outside immediately after I had finished with the last sign.

"Think they'll get the fuckin' message?" Nathan asked as he admired the display.

"We gotta make sure they do." I answered. "If you see anyone cross a cone, shoot'em."

Gino looked at the makeshift barricade and smiled. Eight bright orange construction cones each with a fluorescent orange lettered sign protruding from the top. I think I saw him wipe a tear.

The cones still stood as I left the bar that night. When I arrived the following evening they had been removed (I was hoping that it did not involve the police and a complaint of missing cones. My fingerprints were all over them). Something permanent, or at least semi-permanent, needed to be done to memorialize Charlie. On the next day I visited an antique store on the same block as "Bernie's". I bought an old wooden cane. I painted the cane using a can of gold spray paint I had picked up from work. I also used a drill I found in Louise's garage to drill two holes into the cane, one in the crook at the top and another approximately ten inches from the bottom. I rummaged through Louise's ancient tool box to find a screwdriver and screws to match the holes I had drilled.

With the cane, the screwdriver, and screws I headed to the bar to begin my homage to Charlie.

The front of "Bernie's" was recessed about eighteen inches further from the street than the jewelry store. The area that jutted out at the separation of stores was covered at the corner with wooden trimming. I positioned the cane against this area and screwed it in place into the corner molding. The cane was set somewhere between vertically and diagonally so that the top was directly over the corner, but the bottom extended slightly into the sidewalk area, only a few inches, as a reminder to not pass while smoking. I went into the bar and asked Bonnie, who was behind the bar, for a black "sharpie". I took the pen outside and simply wrote, "Charlie" at the top of the cane. I stepped back to admire my artistic talents. The "Golden Cane" would remain here until vandalized or removed. No, I didn't know him. But from what I had heard, he deserved to be honored.

Randy was not pleased with the cane that had been screwed into the corner of his building. I wasn't even sure if that particular spot was part of his building or the jewelry store's. He walked in from the outside as Sid, Nathan, and I were sitting at the bar that evening. He walked directly toward us, bypassing everyone else at the bar, as if he had something to ask us.

"Do any of you know who put that cane on the building outside?" He asked with a determined look of getting an answer one way or another.

"I did" I answered feeling good about myself, because not only had I honored Charlie, I now realized that this pissed off Randy.

"Yeah, I like it" said Sid, "Al's a regular Michelangelo. All it's missin' is a fig leaf."

Randy was not pleased or amused by our response. "Well it's gotta come down. I don't like it at all and you did damage to my trim by screwing those holes into it. I expect you to fix it." He said with his finger pointing in the direction of the front door.

"It stays, Randy" Nathan said, "If it comes down, we take our drinkin' business elsewhere. I have been comin' in here for twenty years and have spent enough money here to pay for that big house you live in. The three of us together pay your utility bills every month with what we spend. If you wanna lose that, go ahead and take it down. But if you do we will go someplace else to hang out, and you know how many friends I have that come in here. I may not get all of 'em, but I will take as many of them as I can with me." Nathan continued to look Randy in the eye after he had finished. Randy was speechless for a few seconds but kept the determined, angry look on his face.

"I can't have you just putting up stuff on my building without my permission." He said as he pointed to the front door again. "Especially something for an old grumpy man that hated this place."

"Randy" I said, "A dollar ninety-nine tub of spackle and about ten cents worth of paint will repair any damage done to the trim. Can I just buy you a shot and we call it even?"

Randy looked at me with disgust and said, "No thank you." He then stomped away.

Randy was not your typical restaurant owner. The people who visited Bernie's did so despite Randy not because of him. Most business owners are polite and cordial to their patrons. Why would they not be? But Randy would always seem to be pissed off about something every time I saw him. He was not one to walk around the place and welcome people into his establishment with a smile and a handshake.

It was more common to see Nathan walking around the bar and welcoming guests, just as he had done with me. Nathan was a better ambassador for Bernie's than its owner—he along with the friendly bartenders and wait staff. Randy was more apt to walk around and tell you that your barstool was too far into the aisle. Or that a particular spot that someone just sat in is being reserved for someone else—probably one of his golf buddies. He even told Sid once that he was laughing too loud and to keep it down. Sid responded by laughing louder and more often. Randy apparently knew that he was the only game in town when it came to having a drink, and it didn't matter how he treated his customers. The nearest alcohol serving establishment was a twenty minute drive from Pyeville. The town's aversion to building new businesses made it difficult for a new restaurant to open up. He was also now in his mid forties with a middle aged paunchy physique which made it nearly impossible for him to seduce the help anymore. This probably added to his crankiness.

"I hope he don't take it down." Said Sid, "I got no intentions of drivin' all the way to Ricky's Tavern every night. You just wrote a check my butt ain't gonna cash."

"I hope he don't take it down either." Said Nathan, "I was bluffin.'"

~

Since Charlie died the front of his store had been, of course, a lot more quiet. Most everyone still respected the wishes of Charlie and stayed away from his storefront while smoking. Sometimes newbie's or young punks would wander across the imaginary line, the golden cane and puff away. They would sometimes be reminded by a "Bernie's" regular to respect a dead man's wishes and stay on their side. These reminders were not always accepted with an "I'm sorry, I didn't know" but sometimes with a "Fuck you. He's dead." I'll bet Charlie never got a "fuck you." One night, as I was standing outside smoking and well after the jewelry store's closing time, I saw a man approach the front door with keys in hand to unlock it. I walked over toward him.

"Hi." I said as I approached him, "I was very sorry to hear about Charlie. Are you gonna be running the store now?"

The man was dressed in dark slacks with a white shirt and red tie. He was tall, slim, balding, and looked to be around forty-five. He let out a small chuckle.

"Yeah, for a while anyway." he said as he struggled with the door, "My sister and I are gonna share the responsibility until we can find someone permanent"

"You're sister? Are you Charlie's son?"

"Yeah" he said extending his hand, "I'm David Kupp"

"I'm Al, David." I said as I shook his hand, "I'm so sorry. I didn't really know your father but everyone else around here did, and never had anything but nice things to say about him. He will be greatly missed."

David continued to have a difficult time getting the key to unlock the door to the jewelry store. He tried jiggling, pushing, and pulling with no success.

"Daddy, if you are laughing at me while I am trying to get this damn door unlocked, stop it and help me out."

David then effortlessly turned the key and opened the door.

"He did this thousands of times." David said, "He was the only one who knew the trick to getting the key to work. It would have been difficult for someone to break into the place even if they had the key."

"I guess you will eventually find out the trick." I said

"Apparently it's asking the spirit of my father to help. He's still the only one that can do it."

With the door now open, David took a step inside. He then turned around and said to me,

"I just have to get some papers out of his office for my mother. I'm gonna come next door for a beer when I'm finished. Maybe I'll see you in there."

"I'll save you a seat next to me at the bar." I said.

I put out my cigarette and headed back inside. Saving a seat would be no problem because it was after 10:00 and only a few of us remained.

I had been sitting next to Nathan, but as soon as I got back to my barstool he yawned and said, "I'm gonna get outa here. I've had enough."

"K, see ya tomorrow."

"Not if I see you first, bitch."

The pitcher that Nathan and I had been drinking from was empty, so I ordered another from Stephanie along with an extra cold mug for David. I poured myself a glass and focused my attention on the basketball game on TV. It had only been a few minutes when I turned and saw David walk in the front door. He saw me immediately and I waved him over. He approached me with his eyes on the basketball game.

"Who's winning?" He asked as he sat next to me.

"Boston's up by twelve or fourteen. Doesn't matter there's only three minutes left."

David then looked around as if he was seeing the inside of the place for the first time. I poured him a mug full of beer.

"Here ya go" I said, "this pitcher's on me."

"Thanks."

He continued his close inspection of the place from his barstool, checking out the NASCAR paraphernalia on the walls as he rotated his barstool, eyeing the stock behind the bar and the TV's on each end of the room. He turned his mug up, emptying about half and set it back down on the bar. He finally let out a sigh and said, "My dad has been gone for only a few days, and I am inside the place that he hated most in this world. If he had caught me in here when he was alive he would have beaten me to death with that cane of his."

"This your first time in here?" I asked.

"Yeah, for the reason I just mentioned."

Even though I had not invited him in, I felt guilty sitting there next to him. I thought that I should push him out the door for Charlie's sake.

"You still live around here?" I asked.

"Not far. I live in Marietta. I'll be staying here with Mama for a while until we can find someone to run the jewelry store full time."

I suggested she sell it, but she said she couldn't do that to my father. He worked too hard to make it a success for her to just up and sell it after he's gone. She said that after she's gone my sister and I can do whatever we want to with it. Until we can find someone, my sister and I plan to alternate weeks running it."

"How can you spend a week at a time away from home and work?"

"I own a tire store. I don't have to be there every day. My wife is with me here now. The kids are in college. They came in for the funeral, but they're back now. My sister is a nurse and she works a flexible schedule that gives her days off at a time."

"Why did your dad hate "Bernie's" so much?"

"I've known for a long time some of the reasons he despised it. He never liked the idea of alcohol being served next door to his place. He never drank as far as I know. As you probably already know, he didn't like having people smoking so close to his front door. I was surprised when you told me that everyone talked favorably about him. I've seen, first hand, the way he talks to some of the customers from here while they are outside smoking."

"Quite honestly, when I first started coming in here about four months ago," I said, "I saw him one afternoon jabbing at people with his cane nudging them away from his store, and I was shocked that no one got upset about it. They just did as they were told. But after talking to some of the people who knew, Charlie I understood. They said that Charlie had been one of the kindest and gentlest men they had ever known. And away from that sidewalk outside, he was still a kind man. They told stories of how generous he had been to them as kids, giving them candy and other treats for no reason."

"Yeah, that was my dad." He said with a smile.

David then lost his smile and got a serious look on his face. He said to me,

"Spending the past few days here with my mom, I have heard her do a lot of reflecting on my dad's life. I learned some things that I did not know before. And why he really, really hates this place."

"You wanna tell me?" I asked

"I don't wanna bore you, but if you are willing to listen I've been anxious to tell somebody."

"Go ahead. I don't have to be at work for another nine hours."

"My father was a genius. He graduated from high school when he was fifteen years old. It was part genius and part Granddaddy pushing him always to excel in school. He got a full scholarship from Duke University and stayed there until he had finished law school. He did it in five years. He never took summers off. My father was practicing law in Raleigh, North Carolina when he was twenty one years old."

"That's amazing" I said.

"Anyway, that's where he met my mother and they were married. He was working for a pretty large firm and after he had been there a couple of years he had impressed his superiors enough for them to assign him the duties of defending an accused rapist and child molester. My father was excited and jumped in head first determined to win the case. The alleged rapist was a twenty-two years old college student, with a rich daddy, charged with getting a twelve year old girl drunk, beating her, raping her, and throwing her in a trash dumpster behind a grocery store."

"Your dad was how old? Twenty-three?"

"Twenty-three or twenty-four, I'm not sure. Anyway, while

my father was working on the case, he realized that the defendant was guilty. Everything he had been accused of, he did. I don't know if it was a gut felling or he heard something he wasn't suppose to hear, but he knew. Despite that, it was his job to get a 'not guilty' verdict regardless of the man's guilt, that's what lawyers do. Because the young girl was inebriated at the time of the attack, my father reasoned that she could not positively identify him as the one who actually brutalized her. The accused also had some of his friends testify, falsely, that he was not with the girl at the time she had been attacked."

David guzzled down the rest of his beer and poured another.

"Not guilty?" I asked.

"Not guilty. He was found guilty for supplying alcohol to a minor, but served no time. His daddy just paid a fine and took him home."

"But the story doesn't end there." David continued, "Three weeks after this asshole had been let go, the young rape victim hung herself in her parent's basement."

"Damn. What did that do to your father?"

"According to my mother, he was devastated. He had to continue working because, at the time, my mother was pregnant with my sister and he had to provide. He was never the same as a lawyer. But he continued practicing until he was twenty-eight."

"What happened when he was twenty-eight?"

"My grandfather died. At the time of his death, the jewelry store was not very profitable, and the stress more than likely lead to his heart attack. Despite the fact that my father grieved over the loss of his father, he jumped at the opportunity to quit law and take over his father's business. He was excited to be able to move back to his hometown to raise his family and eagerly took on the challenge of making the business profitable again, and he did. My grandfather had earned his business by knowing everyone in town and just trusting that they would come to him for any jewelry needs or repair. My father, however, did something my grandfather never did; he advertised—newspapers, billboards, local radio. This brought a lot of customers in from neighboring towns and the business was very profitable in no time. He also embraced the community and became very involved in his church and civic activities. And maybe because of the guilt he carried for the young rape victim, he adored children and cherished every single encounter he had with them, including my sister and me."

"That's an amazing story. But you still haven't told me why he hated "Bernie's" so badly."

"It is an amazing story but it hasn't gotten weird yet. How's this for an eerie twist of fate? Did I tell you the name of the man my father defended in that rape case?"

"No."

"Bernie Fletcher."

I knew I had heard the name but couldn't remember where. David could tell from my puzzled look that I wasn't following him and started tapping on the bar as if to say, "right here."

"The same Bernie Fletcher that rode into town twenty years ago, got the liquor law changed, and opened this den of iniquity, as my father would say, next to his store."

I was speechless. Over twenty-five years after their days in court, these two were thrown together again, this time on opposite sides. Bernie won both times. And even though Charlie had won his case with Bernie many years ago, he lost both times.

After hearing David's story I thought back to the fit that Randy had pitched about the golden cane. Randy owed his very existence to Charlie Kupp. If my math is correct, Randy was conceived at a time that Bernie would have been in prison serving time for rape, assault, and child molestation. But because of the work of his lawyer, Bernie was free to start a family. Randy Fletcher owed his life to Charlie Kupp and apparently didn't know it.

~

I couldn't get the "Happy Days" theme song out of my head. All day at work I kept stopping myself from mumble-singing, "Monday Tuesday happy days, Wednesday Thursday happy days". I didn't even have the words right but I just kept on singing it to myself all day (The theme actually starts, "Sunday Monday happy days"). I was leaning down behind the counter at my station to get something and as I arose singing, "Goodbye gray skies hello blue" there was a beautiful woman standing in front of the counter waiting for me to re-appear. She had blue eyes, shoulder length brunette hair and was amused by my retro TV crooning.

"Can you tell me where I can find metal shelving?" She asked with a straight face, "Or should I ask the man over in the paint section who's singing the "Beverly Hillbillies" theme?" She then laughed.

I gave her an embarrassed smile and said, "Metal shelving is on aisle nineteen. Bob should be over there to help you. Just follow the sound of the "Rocky" theme, he likes to hum it."

"Thank you" she said with another laugh as she turned to walk away.

111

I admired her as she walked away—a gorgeous body to match the beautiful face.

I arrived at Bernie's that evening, still having visions of Fonzie, Potsie, and Ralph dance in my head. Nathan, Gino, and Sid were already there. I took a seat next to Nathan and looked toward the others as I greeted them.

"Hey guys. What's up?"

Gino responded by yelling, "Phil Collins!"

Merilyn was working behind the bar and there is a game that she likes to play sometimes when the bar is not very crowded. When a song starts playing on the classic rock station that is piped in, if someone can yell out the artist before she can they get a free shot.

"Wrong" said Merilyn, "It's Genesis."

"Same thing" said Gino.

"No it's not" she answered, "He did some things solo and some with Genesis. This is Genesis."

"That's cheatin'. I want my free shot."

"Sorry, my game—my rules."

It was funny to watch this game being played. It was not uncommon to see Merilyn taking a drink order from someone and out of nowhere yell out, "Pat Benetar" leaving those placing their order to wonder what sort of tic was ailing this woman. She was very good at it though. She gave away very few shots.

"Hey" Nathan said, "How was work today?"

"Work's work" I said, "How bout you?"

Sid spoke up, "My job sucks. I have to deal with the stupidest humans on earth. Why can't people learn how to work a fuckin' computer? This man I talked to today actually told me that he couldn't get his desk top computer to come on ever since the power went out. I told him that unless he had a solar powered computer it ain't s'pose to work if there ain't no fuckin' power."

"You said fuckin'?" asked Nathan.

"No, but I damn sure wanted to—the fuckin' idiot."

"Could be worse" said Gino, "You could have one of those jobs of standing on the side of the road, holdin' a sign and wavin' to all the cars that pass by."

"Yeah," I said, "Whatever happened to puttin' the sign on a stick and jammin' it down in the ground, or nailin' it to a telephone pole. Why is it necessary to have somebody holding the sign and dancin' around so that you can't even read it?"

"Sticks are a lot cheaper than payin' somebody by the hour too." Said Nathan.

Merilyn walked over and handed me a mug. "Hey Al"

"Hey Merilyn. How's it goin'?"

Merilyn answered me by yelling, "Blue Oyster Cult!" as she walked away.

Things were sort of quiet. There were only nine people sitting at the bar, including us, and three of the booths were occupied. I grabbed the pitcher as Nathan slid it down to me and poured.

"Where's everybody at?" I asked Nathan.

"I don't know" he said, "but I do know I gotta piss. We had two pitchers before you even got here."

Nathan got up and walked toward the bathroom. Sid looked down at me and asked with a curious look on his face, "Tell me somethin' Al. Why is it that small women are loose and big women are tight?"

"What are you talkin' about Sid?"

"I don't wanna get vulgar here in front of Merilyn." He said.

Merilyn who was now standing in front of us said, "Has my presence ever stopped you from bein' vulgar Sid?"

"You know what I mean Al. Why are big women tight and small women loose down there?" He pointed downward with one hand as he hid it with the other hand trying to shield his motion from Merilyn.

"Maybe there's some sort of medical reason Sid." I answered, "I don't know what to tell ya."

"They're all tight to me." Gino said with a grin.

"That's cuz you're a fuckin' pedophile." Sid quipped.

"You are sick, Sid" Merilyn said, "How do you know that's true about all women?"

"I've been with a few." Sid answered proudly.

"And where are all of these women being treated now?" she asked.

"Chicago!" I yelled.

"Chicago?" Sid asked with a puzzled look, "I've never been to Chicago."

"Chicago is the band that's playin' now." I said as I pointed to the speaker above us. I looked at Merilyn, "I caught you sleepin'. You owe me a shot."

"You set me up." She said in mock anger, "You had Sid lure me into this conversation so that you could swoop in and get a shot."

"Don't question my tactics." I said, "If they work for me, I use 'em. I'll have a shot of tequila please."

"You want trainin' wheels with that?" she asked as she walked toward the shot glasses behind the bar.

"Huh?"

"Trainin' wheels—salt and lime. Or do you wanna take it like a man and just down it?"

"Trainin' wheels please."

Nathan returned from the bathroom with an excited look on his face. He looked as though he had used his bathroom time for other purposes.

"There's two people fuckin' in the bathroom stall." He said as he stood behind his barstool.

"Wha...?" was everyone's response.

"I could hear them back there bumpin' into stuff and moanin' and breathin' heavy."

"Could you tell who it was?" Gino asked.

"I tried to peek through the crack of the door but all I could see was a black dress on the floor." Nathan answered.

"I wouldn't wanna put that dress back on after it's been on the men's room floor." Said Merilyn.

Sid jumped up from his stool and said, "Let's go before they get finished."

"Go where?" I asked, "What are we gonna do?"

"I don't know." He answered, "but I gotta see this."

Sid walked toward the bathroom with Gino, Nathan and I close behind. Merilyn just stood behind the bar shaking her head. When he got to the bathroom door, he turned and gave us the finger over the lips sign as he slowly opened it. The door opened quietly and the three of us followed him in. The pants and moans from behind the stall confirmed Nathan's claim. Sid tried to look through the small crack between the door and the corner of the stall but I could tell by his look of frustration that he wasn't satisfied with the view. No one wanted to look over the top for fear of being seen and then hunted down by the fornicators inside. At that time I was reminded of the camera on my cell phone. Cell phone cameras are often forgotten because the quality of the pictures usually sucks. But at a time like this quality is not that important. We only wanted evidence (for our own enjoyment, not the police) of the day we witnessed live porn at Bernie's. A certain cell phone camera etiquette is implied by those honest people who carry them. You don't use the camera while in a dressing room, in a strip club, at a nudist camp, or in the waiting room of a VD clinic. But when two people are having sex in a public restroom—etiquette shmettiquette—I'm taking pictures.

I pulled out my phone and got the attention of the others. I silently motioned to them my intentions. They all nodded and smiled in agreement. They stepped aside as I held the phone over the opening at the top of the stall and started snapping pictures. The noises from the camera, at first, did not deter the two inside because the noises they were making never stopped. After I had taken six or seven pictures, aiming in all possible directions into the stall, the girl inside screamed and yelled, "Motherfucker!" That was our cue to leave quickly. The four of us left the bathroom and stood against the wall just outside the door.

I put my phone back in my pocket and we stood waiting for them to exit the bathroom. After only a few seconds a young man hurried out the door snapping his pants—shirt untucked and unbuttoned.

"Which one of you was takin' the pictures?" He said angrily as he combed his hair with his fingers.

"I don't know what you talkin' bout." said Sid with an angry look of his own, "We're just waitin' for you two to get finished so we can go to the bathroom."

"Well did you see who just came outa here?" the young man asked, visibly intimidated now by the four of us.

"Some one-armed guy in a red shirt." I said, "He was headed toward the front door."

The young man then hurriedly left to chase down the imaginary man in the red shirt with one arm. We continued to wait outside the door, determined to see who was being violated inside the men's room. The door finally opened slowly and the young woman stuck her head out to make sure no one was around. She was disappointed to see the four of us standing directly in front of her, smiling at her. She was an attractive young woman of around twenty-one. She put her head down and walked out of the bathroom and headed down the hall in her wrinkled partially wet dress. We all gave her a slow clap to parade down the hall to. She ran toward the door when she got to the end of the hall. We then headed back to our barstools to admire the pictures I had taken. As I took my seat at the bar I noticed the song coming from the speaker above me and yelled, "Cheap Trick!"

~

Driving home from work I got a phone call. I looked down to see who was calling.........Flora. I had had no contact with her for over two months. It was after normal closing time at her clinic so I knew that she wasn't at work. I had always talked to her at work before, when she was away from the others. Why is she calling me at a time she would normally be at home with Raymond and the kids? I was excited and scared at the same time. I wanted to hear her tell me how much she missed me and how miserable she was without me.

But I also feared that it was a goodbye of some sort—maybe telling me that Raymond was cured and they were to remarry. I hoped that Raymond was cured, meaning it was time for him to move out and me back in.

I answered enthusiastically, "Hey!"

"Hey" She sounded sad. I could tell she had been crying, "I just wanted to let you know that Raymond died this morning."

Once again, I felt awful for the horrible thoughts that had just gone on in my head.

"I'm so sorry Honey." I said to her, "I'm shocked… It hasn't been that long. I thought he had longer."

"Yeah, me too. He got real bad a couple of weeks ago and just never recovered. He passed away in the hospital in the middle of the night. The kids and I were there to tell him goodbye."

"How are the kids doing?"

"Devastated as expected. Kyle hasn't cried yet, but he also hasn't spoken all day. It's gonna hit him hard at some time, I just don't know when. He's upstairs, alone, playing video games.

For now, I'm just gonna let him deal with it his way. Taylor has been in my arms all day sobbing. She finally passed out from exhaustion and is taking a nap. I wanted to take this time, while she's sleeping, to call and let you know."

To let me know I can move back in? To tell me that it's clear and no one else in the way? Can I now leave the terrible old house and weird people I live with to come back and sleep in the same bed with you again? It's shameful I know, but these are the thoughts that popped into my head. I am selfish and I admit it. I wanted to contact "Miss Manners" to ask her the proper waiting period between ex-spouse's death and old boyfriend moving back in, hoping her answer would be three days.

"Have you made funeral arrangements?" I asked, "I would like to be there for you."

"I have, it's Wednesday at 2:00. But I don't want you there, Honey. With his family there and the kids there it would be awkward."

"Awkward?" I asked, "I would be there for you not his family. You're telling me you don't want me to pay my respects to Raymond?"

"Please…no." she said sweetly "I'm thinking more about the kids. With you there they will be reminded of the time they missed with their father, and I'm afraid the anger they felt toward you before will return and make a tough time even harder on them."

"I understand." And I really did after hearing her explanation. "Is there anything I can do?"

"No, but thank you."

How can I tell her I want to see her? I know that her life is going to be hell for a while longer, but after hearing her voice again, I had to see her. I was never really on my way to being "over" her. I still thought about her often and every day. But I had begun to be little more at ease without her. However, hearing her angelic voice and picturing her in my mind as she spoke, made me want her in my arms.

"I really miss you, Honey." I said. "Can I see you sometime?"

It was probably not the time or certainly not the situation to ask this question, but I just blurted it out.

"I miss you too, but that can't happen for quite a while. I'm sorry, but that's the best way I can answer that. I have a lot to deal with here with the kids and myself and it's just not a good idea right now."

"I understand." I didn't really understand—lunch seemed like a possible time to get together in the near future. But I didn't argue.

"You doin' okay?" she asked.

"Fine" I lied.

"It was good to hear your voice." She said.

"Good to hear yours. I'm sorry it was under these circumstances."

I was sorry about the circumstances. Raymond was younger than me. He did not deserve to die and his family did not deserve to lose him.

"Me too." She said, "I need to run. I'll talk to you later."

I wanted to ask, "when?", but didn't push it.

"Okay, Honey. I'll be thinking about you and the kids."

She said, "You take care now." And she hung up.

I have heard that the opposite of love is hate. I have heard that the opposite of love is indifference. I have heard that love is at the top of the emotional scale and fear is at the bottom, making fear the opposite of love. I don't know which is true, but when it comes to romantic relationships, the opposite of "I love you" is "You take care now". "I love you" means that I want you forever. It means that you are the only one I want to be with. It means the beginning, the middle, and the end. "You take care now" means you are on your own now. I'm not going to be there to help take care of you anymore. It means the end. Those four words echoed through my head as I arrived home. I did not yet know which emotion was stronger inside of me. I was sad for Flora, her kids, and Raymond's family. I was hurt by the finality of the goodbye Flora had given me. I was frustrated because I could not see Flora even though we loved each other. The four words affected me the most—"You take care now".

I went inside, showered, and got dressed. I needed a beer or ten to help me get through the pain that was settling in. I knew that there was a possibility of never getting back with Flora, but those words let me know that hope was almost gone. "You take care now". That's not something you say to someone you plan to spend your life with. "Hang in there" would have been better. At least that could mean good things are on the way. I drove to "Bernie's" with the words repeating themselves over and over in my mind. I took a spot at the bar, alone, and away from everyone. I didn't even look for any one I knew, just looked for an empty barstool. I sat and waited for Stephanie to walk over my way.

"Hey, Al" Stephanie said as she wiped the bar area in front of me. "You not drinkin' with the guys tonight?" She pointed to Nathan and Bobby sitting at the end of the bar.

"Yeah" I said, "If they have a pitcher, just bring me a mug. I'll go over there to fill it."

I knew that I would eventually end up sitting with them. I just didn't want any idle conversation at the moment.

"There's a stool open next to Bobby if you wanna move down there."

"No. That's okay—maybe later."

"Alright, Sweetie, I'll get your mug."

"Thanks Steph."

Stephanie left and returned in no time with a full mug of beer.

"I went ahead and filled it up for ya from their pitcher—saved ya a trip down there."

"Thanks, Steph."

I looked down toward Nathan and saw him looking at me puzzled. He gave me a "what the fuck" look questioning me on why I was sitting alone. I returned his look with a shrug and focused on my beer. I sipped on it slowly, still hearing the words—"you take care now". Am I not important to her anymore? Sure, her kids are more important, but am I nothing now?

Can I not help her get through an emotionally trying time? Isn't that what people you love are around for? I knew nothing that had gone on with her for the past several months. Even when we were talking on a regular basis, it mostly dealt with things at work until I would start off with my whining of loneliness and missing her, which would usually end the conversation. What if she had met someone else—maybe a pharmaceutical rep or a pet owner she encountered at work? Would they rendezvous at the clinic after closing time? Had I been replaced when she realized what a baby I was? She obviously didn't want me anymore. "You take care now" proved it.

"What's up, Bud?" I turned and saw Nathan standing behind

me holding a full pitcher of beer. He set it on the bar and sat beside me.

"Hey" I said, "Not trying to be antisocial, just not in a festive mood."

"Bobby had to leave to look after his wife. Just thought I'd come down and sit with you if that's alright."

"Fine" I said, "Just talked to my girlfriend—ex girlfriend—not quite sure what she is. Anyway, I'm not feeling too good about us right now."

"Whatsa matter?"

I filled my mug and wondered if I should open up and talk to Nathan about this. He knew my general situation, but I had never cried on his shoulder or given him any details. I figured it couldn't hurt. He did ask, after all.

"I've told you the story about her ex husband moving back because he was sick—right? And I had to move out."

"Yeah"

"Well, he died."

"That sucks."

"Anyway, she called me today to give me the news and when she told me goodbye she said 'you take care now."

"That ain't good. You wanted to get back with her didn't you?"

"Yeah—pretty bad." I said.

"No, 'you take care now' ain't good." He said, "Did she give you any idea when you may be able to see her? Did you ask?"

"Yeah, I came right out and asked. She was vague and said she didn't know."

"That sucks. How long were ya'll together?"

"A little over a year."

"A year? Zat all? I've had a longer relationship with the mustard in my refrigerator."

"This was different." I said, "She's perfect. Everything between us was perfect when we were together."

"Nobody's perfect, Romeo. Were you invited to the funeral? You'd have to see her there."

"You don't get invited to a funeral, you just go, egghead. Anyway, I offered to escort her to it and she said it would be a bad idea with his family and the kids there, ya know?"

"Yeah, I guess she would be the grievin' widow—wouldn't be good for someone else who's been bangin' her to be her date."

"Watch it, will ya?" I scolded Nathan, "That's the woman I love, and you don't take a date to a funeral."

"Sorry, Bro." Nathan thought for a second and continued, "Every woman that just recently dumped a man is perfect."

"What are you talkin' about?" I asked.

"Right after you're dumped, all you can think about is all the things you miss about her. You can't think of all the things about her that annoyed you. Think back on all the things about her that bothered you and be glad you are rid of her."

I thought...... I could think of nothing....wait. The only thing I could think of was that Flora had naturally wavy hair, which I loved, and she insisted on running one of those hair irons through it to straighten it. That was it. That's all I could come up with.

"Nothing she did bothered me." I told Nathan.

"She dumped you, didn't she?"

Nathan was trying to help and be sympathetic and I appreciated that. But he wasn't good at it.

~

I couldn't get the last conversation with Flora out of my mind.
It occupied every second of every day. The more I thought about
it the more I was completely convinced that it was over between
us for good. I sensed nothing positive out of it. I felt useless, and
my depression got deeper and deeper with every passing
moment. Drinking wasn't the solution but you couldn't convince
me of that. I continued to visit the bar nightly, but I mostly kept
to myself, away from the others, just like it had all begun there. I
tried to contact Flora at work a week or so after Raymond's
funeral, but she wasn't there. I tried her on her cell phone and got
her voice mail. I did not leave a message, fearing I would start
crying as I spoke. She had to have noticed that I had called. I kept
hoping that she would call me but the call never came. Three
weeks passed and I was ready to die. I wanted to die. Convinced
that I would never be happy again without her, I contemplated
how I was going to end my miserable empty life.

I had a life insurance policy in which Flora was the beneficiary.
I knew that she would take care of Michael financially and she
could also get that pool she had always wanted. I had to find a way

for my death to appear accidental because suicide was not covered. I thought of a few ways to meet my demise without it looking intentional. I briefly considered driving my truck, while not wearing my seatbelt, into a telephone pole at eighty miles per hour. I dropped that notion when I realized that it may not kill me and leave me a slobbering vegetable—or worse yet a fully aware quadriplegic. I also wondered if I could trigger a heart attack on my own. Being a smoker and not exactly an exercise fanatic, I thought if I went for a run in the park, I could just continue to race along the trail until it happened. But I reconsidered this after I thought that the young girl with the hot ass, running in front of me that actually caused my heart attack, would hear me hit the ground and call 911. Paramedics would come, race me to the hospital, save my pathetic life, and leave me with a damaged heart—physically damaged. I had to find a way. I didn't want to suffer. I wanted it to be quick. I was not going to hurt anyone else in the process. To me, life without Flora was no life at all.

~

With something new to occupy my mind, how to die, I was no longer constantly obsessed with Flora. I started to think back on how people I have known died. I had an uncle who was once electrocuted; electrocution may be painful, but I will keep it in mind. A friend's father once died when he fell off a ladder while cleaning gutters; not a sure thing—may just cause injury. A former boss once choked to death; wouldn't know how to go about that. I once heard on the news about a lady who died because her IUD was inserted wrong; mmm…no. I continued to try to come up with something, not thinking it was going to be so difficult to die. I finally found my answer at work.

As I have mentioned before, most of my time at work is spent behind a computer screen at a counter. But every Monday morning I am required to unload a delivery truck using a forklift. We have deliveries Monday through Friday, but Claude, the only other daytime employee that is certified to use a forklift, is off on Mondays. A deadly blow to the head will put me where I want to be—gone forever. How will I do this? I knew that we were receiving a shipment of glass blocks the following Monday. Glass blocks are used for building decorative walls. They are 8" square, 4" thick and weigh 30lbs. per block. Four to a box is how they are shipped, each box weighing 120lbs. I have seen these blocks fall from approximately 20 feet and crack the concrete they land on with no damage to the block. Since I am always alone as I unload the truck, (The truck driver always takes a nap in his cab while I unload) I will easily be able to tamper with the pallet they are stacked on. I will break the band that holds them in place and slide one box very close to the edge. While placing the pallet in the storage rack twenty feet above, a sudden stop will cause the box to fall and I, unfortunately, will unknowingly jump off of the forklift and stand directly beneath it. No way will I survive 120lbs. of solid glass on the head from twenty feet. Merchant's Lumber will be found at fault and Michael should receive a nice settlement from them, through my parents of course, on top of the life insurance.

I still had four days to live. My death had now been planned. For four days I could live as if I were about to die. I'll run my credit cards up to the limit and not worry about paying them off. I'll pull the tag off of my mattress. I emptied my bank account, all $342.00 of it, (Dying with money in the bank, I thought, was like trading in a car with a full tank of gas) and started to think about my last days. I saw myself getting loaded at "Bernie's" of course. But maybe now I can get laid a time or two without feeling guilty about it. Maybe I'll take a drive to someplace I haven't been. I'll call in sick on Friday. What are they going to do—fire me? I also started to think about the world without me. What will it say on my tombstone?

"HERE LIES STEPHEN ALAN SAUNDERS
LOSER, FAILURE, ALCOHOLIC
HE'S NO LONGER TAKING UP VALUABLE
SPACE"

Then I decided that I don't want to be buried. Rotting away in a box underground didn't appeal to me. I would rather be cremated. Then I know at some time or another, maybe a few years down the road, my ashes would end up in a vacuum cleaner bag with paper clips and toenails. That's better than being worm food. But how am I going to let anyone know this? I can't really put a post-it on my forehead that says "cremate me" as the box falls toward my head. What does it matter anyway? Throw me in the ground, burn me, feed me to the sharks—it doesn't matter.

~

My alarm clock woke me up at 6:38 on Friday morning. I rolled over and grabbed my cell phone from the nightstand. I called my boss, Tony, to let him know that I was sick and would not be at work. Calling in sick was something I never did unless I was really ill. Because of this Tony was not upset. He just told me to rest up and he would see me Monday. After making the call I went back to sleep, not wanting to wake up again.

I had wanted to spend this day going for a drive—just following the road with no destination in mind. My plan was to make turns I had never made before and to get lost, just to see where I would end up. But when I woke up at 9:30, I just stayed in bed and turned on the TV. I remember daytime TV being mostly game shows, soaps, and reruns of old programs. Reruns aren't the same as they use to be. "Gilligan's Island", "The Brady Bunch", and "I Dream of Jeanie" have been replaced with recent episodes of every imaginable reality show. I hate reality shows and never understood the public's fascination in watching people suffer. What's the point of these stupid programs?—Strangers thrown together and put into odd, unreal situations which make them grumpy. They end up fighting with one another, making enemies of people they just met, and it's all put together for our entertainment. I was doing enough suffering on my own, and would have preferred to watch Lucy and Ethel get themselves out of a jam concocted by the show's writers. I finally settled on a movie. I didn't know the name. It was an old movie with John Wayne and Dean Martin—totally scripted and not real. I enjoyed those two hours of my day.

After the movie, I turned off the TV and continued to lie in bed. Death was not arriving soon enough. I thought and tried to come up with other ways to die. I came up with nothing new, and decided to stick with my Monday plan at work. However if the opportunity presents itself, I will fall on the grenade to take myself out and save others.

I got out of bed, planning to shower and get out for while. I put on my robe, grabbed my towel and headed down the hall to the bathroom. The door was closed and I could hear the shower running. Albert was in there. For a brief, sick moment I pictured the fat ass all soaped up except for the parts he couldn't reach. With Albert, that had to be most parts—probably why he smelled so bad. Having to put off the shower for a while I headed downstairs to get something to eat. I wasn't hungry but I had an opportunity to steal Albert's food while he was busy—no such thing as a quick shower when there's so much skin to wash. I walked into the kitchen and opened the refrigerator; bologna, olive loaf, sliced processed cheese food, mustard relish—no canned cheese. I lost my desire to eat anything and returned to my room to wait for Albert to finish his hose down. It was almost noon and I was wishing I had gone to work. How was I going to fill the rest of my day?

I flipped the TV back on and was privileged to catch the last fifteen minutes of an episode of "The Family Feud"—"Name something a fat person keeps in his or her refrigerator." My guess is that mustard relish will not be on the board. Shortly after "fast money" I left my room to find that the bathroom was now available. I walked in and tried to check myself out in the mirror but it was still steamed up. I guess I'll shave blindly, careful not to accidently slit my throat. Safety razors suck. With a straight edge I could end my life in a hurry. I looked down at the fish-shaped rubber mats at the bottom of the shower, feeling pity on them for the load they had just endured. I turned on the hot water and let it run for a few minutes trying to sterilize the tub and remove any funk left in there by Albert. When I thought that it was safe with no evil parasites to crawl over me, I jumped in. Sure, I wanted to die, but I didn't want to suffer by being eaten alive from the inside by some blood sucking Albert bacteria. After my shower I went back to my room and got dressed. I decided I would take the drive as I had planned, but cut it a little shorter. I wanted to make sure I had time to visit the bar later and spend some of my "bottom dollars" on getting obliterated. I left my room and headed out. As I passed through the kitchen I opened the cabinet. I was curious as to how many cans of cat food—I mean tuna—were left. Two were missing. That may explain why Louise had been licking herself instead of showering.

I got into my truck, turned left out of the driveway (I had always turned right) and just started driving. I parked in the driveway just to try to get a rise out of Louise. She didn't notice. It wasn't long before I was seeing things I had never seen before—a large field on the side of the road that contained what appeared to be a thousand goats, a billboard picturing a red tractor that read "Get all your farming needs at Myer's feed & seed", an old gas station that had been converted into a tanning salon, more goats, lots of cows, barns, silos, but mostly nothing. Trees, pasture land and an occasional house was all there was. I was getting farther and farther from what was perceived as civilization and deeper into farm and livestock country. Why is a tanning salon needed in farm country? The road was straight with very few bends and my mind wandered toward my upcoming doom. Who will find me lying on the floor in front of the forklift? It could be the truck driver, another employee, or a customer who wanders into the back looking for someone to yell at because they can't find the right color tile grout. I'll have to place something there on the floor, so it will appear that I got off of the forklift to move it—maybe a broom or a buggy. I'm sure the police will come in to investigate the accident. OSHA will get involved. Who will be the first to hear about my death? The name of an emergency contact person is kept in my employee file. I don't remember who it is. I could have changed it to Flora at some time, but if not it's still my ex wife. Either way I'm sure everyone who needs to know will find out soon enough. But will anyone really care?

My parents were kind enough to let me live with them at a time I needed someplace to stay. But I didn't really get along with them that well. As a child I had been terrified of my father. Sometimes he was okay and pleasant to be around, but I never knew when he was going to be in an insufferable mood and chastise me for the smallest little thing. He once got angry at me and called me stupid because I didn't know who the vice-president was—I was eight. I never knew if a spilled drink was going to bring about a calm, "go grab something to clean it up", or a backhand to the face followed with, "be more careful, you idiot!" I got the occasional whipping, but the words and the way in which they were delivered did the most damage. Mood altering medications could have done him a world of good, but my father was convinced that he was the only sane person alive and the rest of the world was wacko. My mother was good to me, for the most part, but I believe she was also afraid of him. She never intervened on my behalf during one of his rants. I believe that the two of them didn't want children. I have to assume that I was a mistake, being born during their late thirties, and was not necessarily a welcome addition. I'm sure they'll be a little saddened by my death, but at their age, I'll see them again soon.

Michael will be hurt by my death. But at eight, his memories of me are mostly every other weekend visits, not every day life with Dad. He hasn't had enough time with me to miss me terribly. Any memories of his mother and I living with him as a family would have to be vague. His mother has been seeing a nice man for almost a year now. I love this little boy more than anything but he will be a much better father for Michael than I ever could. By the time he is an adult, I will be long gone and long forgotten. My friend's at "Bernie's" will hear about my accident and talk about it at the bar. But any sadness they may feel can be drowned by another round. The people at work will be stunned for a short while. But they'll just go through the applications they keep on file for six months and have me replaced in a week.

What will my death do to Flora? In a short period she will have lost an ex husband and an ex live-in lover. Maybe this will teach her to hold on to the next guy. I'm sure her kids will throw a "going away forever" party for me. I don't want Flora to suffer or blame herself. But she will probably just attend the memorial service and then move on with her life; sipping cocktails by her new pool with a pharmaceutical rep. Any way you look at it my life is meaningless and my absence from this world is not going to have a "George Bailey" affect on anyone.

After driving for a little more than an hour, I arrived in a town called Chaffin. I'd never heard of it, much less been there. The town consisted of a four-way stop and a small convenience store on that corner—at least that's all I saw. If Elvis was alive and wanted no one to know, this was a good place for him to live. I was out of cigarettes so I pulled into the store to buy a pack. I got out of my truck and walked in. I was greeted by an elderly lady behind the counter.

"Aftanoon" she said through her three remaining teeth.

I ignored the greeting and walked toward the coolers to get a drink. I then realized that this was the first American convenience store clerk I had seen in a long time—if you want to call her American. I was in such strange surroundings I felt as though maybe I had left the country. I grabbed a Dr. Pepper, returned to the counter and set it down. The lady was smiling a gapped tooth smile eager to help out the city boy—probably not accustomed to her customers wearing shoes and store bought clothes.

"'at gonna do it fer ya?' she asked.

"Gimme a pack of Marlboros." I said.

"Box or soft?"

"Box."

"Red or light?"

"Red."

I usually smoked the lights, but why bother now? Cancer isn't going to kill me, I am.

"Got a three—pack special fer nine eighty—nine."

"Just one."

"Ya wanna get a lottery ticket? Jackpot's up to over a hunnert million."

"No" I said, "I'm a big loser."

I paid her and left. I had seen enough of the countryside and decided to head back home. It was almost three o'clock, unless I entered another time zone, and I didn't want to waste any more of the day in "Hazard County."

~

Driving only an hour outside my normal "comfort zone" I was reminded of how things were when I was a child. I grew up only thirty miles from Atlanta, but the surrounding areas had not grown to the size they are now and it was still very rural. All of the kids and adults that I grew up around were born in the south and knew only one way to speak—incorrectly. Taking English classes in grammar school was like learning an entirely different language. With my deep southern drawl I could have won the part of one of the kids in "To Kill a Mockingbird". Food wasn't food unless it was fried, shoes were absolutely not necessary if the temperature was above 65 degrees, and the neighborhood pool was a spot in the creek that we dammed up with rocks, logs and any other debris we could find. At the beginning of the school year, as I was entering the fifth grade, I met a boy who had just moved from Ohio. He talked very funny. He actually talked normal, but differently than all the other kids at Hardy Elementary School. He was an outcast from the beginning because he could not understand us and we could not understand him—not just the words we spoke, but the things we spoke of. He didn't know what grits were. We thought a bagel was a type of "huntin' dawg". He eventually became friends with a boy who moved in from Illinois during the school year. They both got A's in English. Each school year thereafter more and more kids showed up from other parts of the country. I became friends with many of them and eventually removed the phrase "fixin' to" from my vocabulary. As an adult I became completely "yankeefied" when it grew to be easier to find an Indiana native around me than someone who actually grew up here, like me. Working with the public, as I have done throughout my professional career, forced me to lose most of my southern accent and expressions because I felt it made me seem less intelligent than others. It became hard for new people that I met to believe that I was a native of Georgia.

"But you don't have an accent." They would say.

"We've been speaking English here in Georgia for hundreds of years." I would answer.

Anyway, the drive to Chaffin reminded me that I'm not that far away from where I use to be. I was looking down my nose at the city and its surroundings, but if not for a population explosion of the Atlanta area years ago, I may still be living in such a place. I wanted to drive back and give the lady in the convenience store a hug. She probably would have liked that.

~

After stopping at home for a bathroom break, a snack, and to blow my nose on one of Albert's clean shirts (he had left his clothes in the dryer, and I wanted to put one of mine in to get the wrinkles out), I jumped back in my truck and headed to "Bernie's". Friday night would be busy, so I got there early to make sure I would have a seat at the bar. I walked in and grabbed a barstool near the front door and away from the stage in the back. It was 5:30 and the band would be starting up at around 8:30. I was not interested in having a good view of the forty-something's pretending to be teen idols. The bands that played here did have their following of groupies. As far as I knew, these groupies did not work in a seafood restaurant but would serve crabs to anyone interested. Joanie was behind the bar. She noticed me and strutted my way.

"Wanna beer Al?" she asked.

"Yeah" I said, "and a shot of Jack."

She gave me a strange look before she turned and walked away. I had always drunk beer only. But tonight I was ready to get polluted. When she returned with my drinks, I grabbed the shot and downed it before she could leave again.

"Another one please" I said as I caught my breath.

"You okay, Al?"

"Fine."

She gave me another strange look and walked away to get my shot. I knocked back half of my beer while waiting for my shot. Joanie returned quickly and set the glass in front of me. I repeated the act again and asked for another.

"I'm not doin' this all night, Al." she said as she rolled her eyes, "What's up? You tryin' to kill yourself?"

I ignored the question. If only she knew. I looked around the place to see who was there—some familiar faces but no one I generally sat with. As usual, men outnumbered women three to one. But when the band starts playing the ratio will tighten. Women tend to show up when there's dancing involved. Joanie returned with my third shot of Jack, set it on the bar and quickly turned and walked away before I could down it and ask for another. As she was taking the order of someone else several stools down from me I yelled over to her, "Now I need another beer."

"Slow down, Al." she yelled back, "I'll be back in a minute. It ain't nowhere near closin' time. You got all night."

Not knowing when my next drink would come, I decided to sip on the Jack this time. Looking around the bar again I remembered my promise to Flora that I would be faithful to her. Flora, now, had no interest in me and I was sure did not give a damn if I kept that promise or not. I don't know if the promise ever meant anything to her. I had been nothing in her life for eight months now and she was certainly in no hurry to welcome me back in. "You take care now" translates into "fuck anybody you want to".... So that was my plan.

I started conducting a "Bernie's Beauty Contest" in my mind. There were only seven women in the place. Four were sitting in booths with men. The other three were sitting at the bar—two of them with men. The one woman sitting alone was fairly attractive but probably too young for me—not really, but I'm sure I was too old for her. She appeared to be around 25. I didn't rule out the ones that were with men. Often times I have seen these situations end up not looking as they appear. Sometimes it's just an old friend, sometimes it's a relative (that may not matter in some southern states), and sometimes it's not explained—the man just leaves alone. I wasn't ready to pounce yet. It was still early. I just wanted to get an early peek at the menu—sounds crude I know, like choosing a cow at a cattle auction, but women do it too. There will be more to choose from later. The genders will balance out once the band starts. I'll keep drinking, therefore lowering my expectations.

"Dare I ask?" Joanie was standing in front of me with her hands on her hips.

"Yeah, Sweetie" I said "One more of each."

"If you keep this up, Al, we will be carryin' you outa here. Are you sure you okay?

"I'll be fine as long as I keep drinking and I can't keep drinking if you don't bring them to me. So it's up to you to make sure I'm fine." I was already starting to feel the effects of the Jack. I'm not use to hard liquor.

"Okay, but I do have the right to cut you off when that time comes."

"I'll be okay, just let me drink."

Joanie obliged and brought me more booze. I had hoped that I would run into Jan. Jan is "hot" and had wanted me from the time we first met. I continually came up with reasons not to go home with her because of my obsession with Flora. If I see Jan tonight it's a sure thing. But I couldn't count on seeing her. It had been a while since she had been at the bar. I downed the shot and without hesitating downed the beer. The fourth Jack and second beer had now been emptied and I needed a trip to the bathroom. I called out to Joanie and when she looked at me I raised my empty mug and my empty glass. She gave me a look of concern and nodded. I got up from my stool, tipped the stool against the bar (That's the symbol of "this seat is taken") and started for the men's room. I was feeling brave now. The drinks were starting to kick in and turn me into a suave, smooth-talking lover. I was still able to walk straight and as long as I could remain conscious, I liked my chances. I took care of business in the bathroom, checked myself in the mirror, washed my hands and wondered why there was a sign in front of me telling me how to properly wash my hands. If I don't know how to wash my hands I probably can't read. As I reached my seat the drinks were there waiting for me, and so was a brunette who had taken the stool next to me. I hadn't really noticed her before I sat. I was watching the door to see who was walking in as I approached the barstool, so it was difficult to check her out since she was so close. The only way I could do that was turn and look directly at her—not easy to hide that when she's right next to you.

I threw back the shot and sat the glass down on the bar. I then reached for my beer and as I went to take a sip, she spoke.

"Hi. I noticed you from the other side of the room and you looked lonely—thought I'd come over and say hello. My name's Barbi."

Barbi is the name of a stripper. Barbi is the name of someone you don't marry but have unbelievable sex with. Barbi will do things that will cause a porn star to blush. Barbi is sitting next to me and wants to meet me. Perfect! I turned to look at her and recognized her as one of the women I had seen earlier sitting with a gentleman in one of the booths.

"Hi Barbi, I'm Al."

I looked over to the booth where she had been sitting and noticed that it was empty. Her companion had apparently left.

"I noticed you too." I said, "Weren't you sitting with someone over there earlier?" I pointed toward the booth.

"Yeah, that was my boss. He brought me here to discuss business after work. I could tell he had other intentions so I told him that you were my boyfriend and I had called you to meet me here for drinks."

"So we just met, and already I'm committed." I said, "what if he had said he wanted to meet me?"

"He had just invited me back to his place, so meeting my boyfriend was the last thing he wanted to do."

I could at last look at her. She looked to be in her mid thirties, brown eyes, shoulder length brunette hair—attractive but not a knock out. I called Joanie over once again.

"I'll have one of each and Barbi will have a…"

"A Jaeger and a beer." She said.

Good. She wants to get wasted too. The drinks came and we emptied them quickly. Then we did it again. Joanie obliged without incident, either not wanting to embarrass me in front of my new friend or perhaps thinking Barbi could get me home safely….I didn't get home at all that night.

I woke up with a pounding headache. I got out of bed and started toward the bathroom. Why am I naked? I felt my pants under my feet so I picked them up and slipped them on. I was rubbing my temples with one hand, covering my eyes when I bumped into something. Who put a make-up table in my bedroom?… This isn't my bedroom…. Where am I?

The streetlight was shining into the room and I looked around confused, taking in my surroundings. There was someone else in the bed. The clock on the nightstand read 4:32. Things started to come back to me a little. I still had to pee so I opened the door and staggered out of the room and into the hall hoping the bathroom door would be obvious. There was a door to my right that was slightly ajar. I pushed it open and reached for a light switch. I flipped on the light and saw a familiar sight. At some time in the past few hours I had definitely hurled into that toilet.

I vaguely remembered Barbi's face. I had finally gotten laid and I can remember nothing about it. I knew I had because when I pissed it went in all different directions. It must have been okay. She didn't make me sleep on the floor. She was still in bed with me when I woke up. I finished, washed my hands, turned out the light and headed back to the room. Even though I felt like shit, it was good to see someone else in bed that I could snuggle next to for a change. I removed my pants and got back into bed. She was on her side with her back to me so I slid next to her and put my arm around her, placing my hand on her breast giving it a gentle squeeze. I began to remember more of her as I had sat next to her at the bar. Even in my current condition I wanted more—at least something I could remember. She awoke just as I had hoped she would. She let out a quiet sensual moan and reached her arm around and placed it on my thigh giving it a squeeze. She then turned over on her back ready to get things started again. I pressed against her and moved in for a kiss.......Joanie!?

~

"You ready to go again, Stud?" Joanie asked in a sleepy hoarse voice.

I couldn't believe it. How did I end up with Joanie? I couldn't remember a thing concerning her, except that she was behind the bar last night. I was sitting with an attractive woman. From what I can remember we were getting along well and having some laughs. What happened to her? I'm in bed with Joanie. I had seen her working at the bar on many occasions before, but I never looked at her in any sexual kind of way. She's not unattractive— just not someone I would normally have interest in. What? How? Why? She called me "Stud". I must have done something right. How am I going to answer her question? Do I want to go again? I do want to go again—but with Joanie? Should I ask her what happened last night? Would letting her know that I have no recollection hurt her feelings? I decided that since I have only two days to live and this may be the last woman I will ever be with……. yeah. Why not? I'll go again. At least then asking what happened last night won't hurt her if I show that I am willing now.

"And again after that" I answered.

"Might need a nap after this one, but we'll go again when I wake up if ya wanna."

I proceeded from where I had stopped, still pressed closely against her I leaned in and kissed her. "Middle of the night" breath be damned—we kissed passionately then moved on to other things. After I had finished and Joanie had finished three times, I lay next to her with my arm around her and fell back asleep.

I woke to sunlight hitting me in the face. I looked across the bed to the clock and saw that it was 9:26. Joanie was not there. I had to pee again so I got out of bed and slipped on my pants. I walked out the door and to the bathroom. The door was closed but not locked. I opened it and as I started to walk in I was stopped by the sight of a little boy with his pajama pants pulled all the way down to the ankles, butt exposed, standing on his toes peeing into the toilet. He apparently didn't hear me because he didn't turn around. Without completely shutting the door back I quietly retreated to the bedroom I had just left. I sat on the bed, afraid to leave the room again. I didn't know if being spotted by the boy was something I should try to avoid. Where was Joanie? How long am I going to have to sit here alone in a strange place?

I got up and walked to the window. For the first time I was able to clearly see this place that I had been blindly taken to the night before. I was on the second floor of what appeared to be an apartment building. There were a few people moving about outside. I saw a lady carrying her laundry in a basket and a gentleman entering his car directly below me. What I thought was a streetlight the night before was a parking lot light. The apartment buildings formed a "U" shape. There were buildings straight across from me and to my right. They were three stories high and all painted a putrid shade of green. I saw no clubhouse or pool. It appeared to be a low-rent, slightly run-down complex.

To my left was the street. What street, I didn't know. Are we still in Pyeville? Are we fifty miles away? I had never heard Joanie talk about where she lived. I turned to inspect the bedroom. A queen-size, four post bed was centered against the wall and across from the door. On each side of the bed was a two-drawer nightstand, each with a small lamp, which matched the bed's dark cherry wood color. Against the wall, opposite the window, was a white make-up stand next to a small mirrored dresser that matched the bed also. The closet was beside the door, to the left. It was a small two sliding door closet. One door was open and clothes spilled out if it at the bottom. The floor was gold shag carpet and the walls were white. The only thing hanging on the wall was directly above the bed. It was a picture of Joanie, sitting with a little boy standing on the right side of her and a little girl, slightly older than the boy, on the left. The boy, I would guess, is the same boy I had just seen. I couldn't tell for sure, his butt wasn't showing in the picture. Still dressed in just my pants I laid on the bed and stared at the ceiling—white stucco with no overhead light or ceiling fan. Where is Joanie? I still have to pee and I don't know if I can leave the room.

I heard voices outside the room. They weren't right outside the door but I could hear some muffled conversation going on somewhere in the apartment. It was Joanie and a man. I couldn't make out what they were saying, but the exchange appeared to be a little heated. What have I gotten myself into? I also didn't know Joanie's marital situation. None of the bartenders wear wedding bands, but I know that Merilyn and Bonnie are married. They don't wear them because of the risk of losing them behind the bar, or in the sink. Is it her husband? Was he away for the weekend and show up unexpectedly? Maybe I'll die sooner than expected and it actually won't be suicide. Maybe he has a gun and is ready to use it on the slimy dog that's doing his wife. I hope he doesn't hurt

Joanie or the kids though. There was no evidence of a man living here. All the clothes I saw pouring out of Joanie's closet were women's. The voices stopped and I heard a door slam. The bedroom door opened a few seconds later and Joanie walked in. I sat up quickly not knowing what to expect. She looked at me smiling.

"Okay" she said as she removed her robe, exposing to me that there was absolutely nothing underneath the robe, "I promised you another."

The robe fell to the floor. She walked to the bed, pushed me down on my back and straddled me while she reached down to unsnap my pants. I now looked at Joanie sexually for the first time. Her brown hair was hastily pulled back in a pony-tail. Her make-up from the night before was smudged; black stuff flaked beside each eye. Her brown eyes were bloodshot. She had a tattoo of an eagle on her left tit—good thing I'm not picky at this point. She kissed me and I kissed back, but I pushed her over to her side and I lay on my side beside her. We separated lips.

"Okay, but let's talk first." I said.

"Bout what?"

"I have gotta pee."

"Go pee." She said, "I'll be here waitin' for ya."

I returned to the room and as she had promised, she was waiting on the bed. I removed my pants and crawled in beside her. We got under the sheets. She leaned in to kiss me and I stopped her.

"Having to pee wasn't all I wanted to talk about." I said.

"What's on your mind?"

"I just heard you arguing with someone. Should I be here?" I asked.

"That was my ex. He was supposed to pick up the kids last night while I was at work. He never showed up so the babysitter had to stay here until I got home at 1:30. I didn't find out until I got here, otherwise you would not have come home with me. But after I had you here I had nothing else to do with you, so I just did ya. Anyway, he gave me some story about car problems and I asked him for the extra money I had to pay the baby sitter, he didn't wanna give it to me…blah blah blah. That's why we were arguing. You actually belong here more than he does right now. He should have come last night so that I wouldn't have to look at him."

"Oh….. About last night—what happened?"

"You don't remember anything?"

"I remember I was sitting next to some woman I had just met—Barbi. We were drinking shots and beer—next thing I remember is its 4:30 and I'm in bed with you."

"You remember nothin' else?"

"That's it." I said.

"I could tell you were toasted, but I gotta tell ya, you carry yourself pretty well to be so far gone that you remember nothin' and still be able to walk and talk, not to mention fuck."

"Thank you…I think."

"Well" she said, "You and the Barbie doll had several shots with beer. I would have cut you off but I didn't want to embarrass you and spoil any chances you may have with her. So I just told myself that if the two of you got so far gone that you couldn't drive home I would take you both home—whether that be your place or her's. At some point, you asked for another round and I told both of you that before I would serve you any more I had to have your car keys. You both obeyed and gave them to me. I thought that I would be coming home to an empty apartment so I was in no rush to get here. You two seemed to be getting along well and despite the amount you had had to drink you were both behaving and not being obnoxious. But shortly before closing time—maybe around 12:30, Barbi fell asleep with her head on the bar."

"No shit?"

"No shit. Randy came over and saw her and tried to wake her up. He couldn't wake her up so he said we would have to call her a cab to take her home. I then told Randy that if we call her a cab there is no way we will know where to send her if she can't tell us where she lives. You then spoke up and said, 'she's with me, I'll take care of her.'"

"I don't remember saying that."

"You did. Well Randy said, 'if she's with you, you gotta get her outa here now'. You then said, 'but I ain't ready to leave'. So Randy said, 'If she's with you, you gotta get her outa here. After you get her outa here, I don't care what you do'. I told Randy that I would take care of it and he went back to his office. I took the keyless entry off of your key ring and handed it to you. You were able to get her awake enough to walk her outside. You took her to your truck and set her inside and then you came back in."

"I did all that?"

"You then sat at the bar through "last call" and closing until I had finished all I had to do to leave. You made a few trips out to your truck to check on her, but I was not going to let you drive anywhere. I kept the keys."

I vaguely remembered some of the things Joanie was telling me, but it was like trying to remember a weird dream, or like something I had seen in a movie a long time ago.

"I wonder if she threw up in my truck." I said, "So how did I end up here?"

"When we left, you walked out and got in my car and we drove over to your truck to get Barbi. We sat her in the back and I asked her where she lived. She couldn't speak. She tried to tell me but she was slurring so badly I couldn't understand her. I then asked you if she could stay with you and you said that any unusual noise would upset your landlady and cause you to get evicted. I didn't know what else to do, so here we are."

"You mean…?"

The bedroom door opened and Barbi peeked her head in. She saw us in bed and at first looked embarrassed, but while trying to avert her eyes asked, "Where am I?"

She had been here the whole time. The woman that I thought I would end up with last night was actually with me last night, I just didn't know it. Here I am in bed with Joanie as she stands in front of us. She still looks good even with her tousled hair and wrinkled clothes.

"You're at my apartment, sweetie." Joanie answered. "You couldn't tell me where you lived last night and I couldn't exactly leave you in the parking lot."

Barbi now had the courage to look straight at us and enter the room. Joanie and I were both under the sheets so no vital parts were exposed.

"I'm sorry." Barbi said, "I had no intentions of getting so wasted. Whose room was I in?"

"That was my daughter's. I just put her in bed with my son so that you could get some rest."

"Thank you so much. I don't even know you. That was a sweet thing to do."

"It was my pleasure." Joanie said with a smile, "but if you wanna repay me I know something you can do."

"Anything"

"Hop in bed with us."

She undressed and did just that.

~

I arrived home at about 3:00 in the afternoon. Joanie took Barbi and me back to "Bernie's" to pick up our vehicles. The apartment complex where she lives, it turns out, is just on the edge of town only a few minutes away. The morning and early afternoon had been quite an erotic adventure. Every man should have the experience of being with two women at once before he dies. I made it just in time. However, I would have traded hundreds of these experiences for one more night with Flora. The previous few hours had been very enjoyable, but it wasn't what I wanted. I still wanted to die. I walked in the house to find Louise sitting at the kitchen table. She was eating something—tuna perhaps. She looked up at me from her seat.

"You musta had a rough night." She said with a concerned stare, "You look awful."

"Yeah. I got arrested for exposing myself to school children—spent the night behind bars in the arms of a guy named Butch"

"You're such a smart ass." She said with a chuckle, "I bought some hanging baskets today. Will you please hang them on the front porch for me?"

"Sure. Where they at?"

"The trunk of my car. It's open." She answered.

I retreated and went back outside to hang the plants. As I was getting them out of the car I saw Sue coming out of her door in the back. She was in her work uniform. Sue normally worked the morning shift at the pancake house—maybe she swapped shifts with a co-worker. She saw me and waved—I waved back. She then got in her car and left. I grabbed two handles in each hand and carried the four baskets around to the front of the house. I placed the handles on the hooks that hung from the front porch and went back inside. I was exhausted and needed a nap. After a couple of hours of sleep I planned to shower and head to "Bernie's"—just beer tonight.

Falling asleep would be no problem. I was still a little hung-over and had slept only a few hours the previous night, not to mention the unusual amount of physical activity that I had not been accustomed to for a long while. I undressed, threw my well-worn clothes into the hamper and slid under the covers. I set my alarm for 6:15. That will give me time to shower and arrive at the bar at around 7:30. The bed felt good. It was quiet, and as I was about to drift off I was awakened by Louise talking loudly on the phone. She was still in the kitchen, downstairs, but her voice carried throughout the house. I wanted to jump out of bed and run down to tell her that I needed to sleep and she was disturbing me (or write her a note and stick it in her face). I don't care if it's the middle of the afternoon; being quiet at 3:00 made as much sense to me as being quiet at 8:30. But in order to avoid a confrontation, I waited patiently for her to finish her phone call to fall asleep. If she wakes me up again, I'll put marijuana seeds in her new hanging baskets. I know where to get them. Drinking is not all they do at "Bernie's."

The sight of pot growing on the front porch, for all to see, is sure to draw attention. Too bad I wouldn't be around to see how that turns out, if it was necessary. As it turned out, pot seeds were not necessary. I fell asleep with no trouble.

~

I awoke and shut off my alarm. It took me a few seconds to make sense of the situation. It was still daylight out and I don't normally get up at 6:15 in the afternoon. I lay in bed briefly, trying to recall why I was in bed at this hour. It is almost never a good sign to wake up in your own bed and not remember why you're there. The events of the past twenty-four hours then started to replay in my mind—at least those hours that I could remember. As much as I thought I had enjoyed my tryst with Joanie and Barbi, I felt horribly guilty for what we had done. Other men would kill to be in the situation I had been in, but I regretted every second of it now. Even though I was prepared to end my life in a little more than a day, I felt as though I had betrayed Flora. As far as I knew she was already in the arms of another man—maybe, maybe not—I had no way of knowing for sure. But she was the only one I wanted, and my perceived betrayal made me hate myself even more.

I needed to drink. I got out of bed, put on my robe and headed to the shower.

It was almost 8:00 when I arrived at the bar. Bonnie was

working which made me feel good. Facing Joanie would have been awkward to say the least. The only open barstool I found was directly in front of the stage. That sucked because the band would be starting up in half an hour and I didn't have enough time to get drunk before they got started. Bonnie came over to me and stood on her toes as she placed a coaster in front of me.

"Wanna beer, Al?" She asked.

"Yes, please."

"I hear you had a pretty good time last night." She said with an evil smile.

"Whataya mean?" I asked.

"Joanie came in earlier to pick up her tips from last night. For some reason she left in a hurry and forgot to pick them up." Bonnie then walked away, still smiling. "I'll be right back." She said over her shoulder.

If Bonnie knows I can imagine that everyone in here knows by now. This shouldn't bother me. Why would I care? I'll go out like a rock star. Everyone will say, "Remember Al? He's the one that did Joanie and another woman at the same time one night." I'll be a hero......A dead hero. I just hope nothing is said around Flora about this at the funeral—wouldn't want her to find out. Even in death, I wanted her to think that I remained faithful to her. Am I being too optimistic to even think that any of these people will show up at my funeral? Am I being optimistic to think that Flora will show up at my funeral? Am I even worthy of memorializing at all?

Bonnie returned with my beer, "Here ya go, Stud" she said still grinning as she set the mug in front of me. "How ya feelin' tonight? I'll get off at one—or whenever you help me do so. Go ahead and pick us out one. Make sure you get a pretty one with big boobs."

I was not sure how to feel about her comments. Apparently

Joanie was proud of what she had accomplished the night before, but I wasn't sure that I was comfortable with everyone knowing or of what Joanie may be expecting from me now. I'll be okay as long as I don't run into her before Monday morning.

"What do you know exactly?" I asked Bonnie.

"Joanie just told me that she took you and some other woman home with her last night. She didn't give me any details but I can fill in the blanks myself, unless you wanna fill them in for me."

"Sure." I said, "We stayed up most of the night reading poetry to each other and then we had a pillow fight and fell asleep on the floor in our pajamas."

"Thanks Al, but I'm gonna keep the images I had in my head before."

Bonnie then walked away to take care of some of the other drunks. I sipped on my beer and looked around the place to see who was there. When I had first arrived I just looked for an open stool without noticing who was in the occupied ones. Nathan and Frank were sitting on the far side of the bar, near the front door. I waved over to get their attention. When Frank finally saw me I gave him the sign to save me a stool if one becomes available near them (The sign cannot be described—barflys just know it). I finished my beer and called out to Bonnie. She walked over to me.

"I'll have another please." I said.

"You got it, Casanova. Don't drink too much. I wanna make sure you can still get it up later."

Bonnie was clearly just busting my chops. She is happily married and has two small children. I had met her husband and the kids when he visited her once while she was working. As guilty as I had been feeling about what I had done, the positive attention that Bonnie was giving me started to make me feel a little better about myself—maybe what I did wasn't so bad. She returned with my beer.

"Hey Bonnie." I said as she struggled to reach my side of the bar with the mug, "Joanie's not thinking that there is anything happening between us is she? I mean, she's not looking for a boyfriend—right?"

Bonnie laughed, "Do you think that you are the only drunk she has ever left here with? Trust me, she don't want no relationship."

"Good" I said, embarrassed now, "Just wanted to be sure."

"The thing about this that made it different—another woman was involved. Joanie didn't tell me much, I was really busy when she came in, but I believe she really enjoyed that part. She will bed a man once in a while but she hates men for the most part. She takes so much shit from them when she's here she's turned off by them. She uses them for one thing, one time and that's when she's damn good and ready. I've never seen her accept an invitation from one of her customers to go home with them. She picks who she wants and usually gets who she wants. Last night opened up new doors for her though. She's doubled her prospect list."

"Does anyone else know?" I asked her.

"Don't worry. Joanie's my best friend." She said, "We tell each other everything, but it won't go any further."

I gave her a smile and a wink and she responded with a smile and her tongue sweeping across her upper lip—still busting my chops.

I looked up to see Nathan waving me over his way. A stool had opened up next to him. The timing was perfect because the band was starting to tune up their instruments. I grabbed my beer and walked away from the sound checks and "Rolling Stones" riffs.

"Hey Nathan…Frank"

"Hey Bud" Nathan said as he turned around, "Thought you got too good for us—never sit with us anymore."

I took my seat next to Nathan, "Damn sure not too good." I said, "Just been broodin' for the most part."

157

My southern accent came back to me often when I talked to a fellow southerner. I felt as they I didn't have to hide it around them.

"Whatcha broodin' about?" asked Frank.

"Relationship stuff—don't wanna talk about it tonight." I answered, "I'm done with it."

"Good" said Nathan with a grin, "we damn sure don't wanna hear it."

At that point I decided that this night was going to be spent as most of my nights had been spent here—drinking beer and talking with my friends. We were later joined by Sid and his wife, Lorie. I had my usual amount—enough to get drunk but not enough to forget anything. We made fun of the band, made fun of each other, made crude comments to Bonnie about her height ("Hey Bonnie, you can improve your tip if you wanna go up on me"), and we laughed until it hurt. We stayed until closing time and then each went our separate ways. Outside the doors of "Bernie's" my hurt returned and it wasn't from the laughter. I would be dead in thirty-six hours. I could hardly wait.

~

I made it home and parked in the street in front of the house. It was a nice warm June night so I lit up a cigarette and decided to take my time getting inside. I looked up at the stars wondering what life after death was really like. I would enter the spirit world, but what does the spirit world entail? Would I float around earth able to watch others without being seen? Could I make myself known if I chose to? Or would Whoopi Goldberg be the only person who could hear me?

Maybe my spirit would be in another dimension, another plane far from this world. My beliefs about life after death had changed drastically since I was a kid. Good people go to heaven, bad people go to hell. That's what I had been taught. I definitely would not consider myself a good person, but I wasn't exactly a serial killer. But if God is the loving Being that most people say He is, why would there be a hell? Punishment is one thing, but a fiery pit to spend eternity in seemed like overkill for someone who may have spent their life as a kleptomaniac. I will find out soon enough.

As I walked around puffing on my cigarette I noticed that

Sue's car was not parked in the back. The pancake house is open twenty-four hours. It was 1:15 and she was obviously still at work. I stomped my butt into the driveway and walked inside. I was careful not to make too much noise. I didn't want to receive another note from Louise and spend my last full day on earth pissed off at her. The stairs creaked as I climbed them. I winced with every step trying to tread as lightly as possible. I made it to my room and closed the door without a sound. I undressed and got into bed. Despite the fact that I had woken from a nap only a few hours earlier, the beer I had consumed since would help me to fall asleep quickly. I thought about how I would spend my last day as I lay on my side. I had no plan and fell asleep before I could come up with one.

I was awakened from a deep sleep by someone tapping me on the back. Startled that someone else was in my room, I spun around quickly to see who was there.... It was Michael. I rubbed my eyes in disbelief. How did he get here? He stood there beside my bed holding his stuffed "Spongebob", wearing his light blue "Spongebob" footy pajamas. His brown hair was mussed as if he had just crawled out of bed.

"Daddy, wake up." He said as he continued to poke me, even though I had turned over.

"What are you doin' here Sport? How did you get here?" I asked him, still confused.

"Daddy, we have to go back to the zoo." He said in a shaky voice, as if he was fighting back tears.

"Okay Sport. We'll go back to the zoo. What's wrong?"

"We have to check on the penguins. The penguins are in trouble. It's too warm for them at the zoo. We have to save them."

"The penguins are fine—remember? We saw them not long ago."

"No Daddy. They're not okay. Their goin' to die. We have to save them." He was starting to cry.

"Okay son, we'll go back to the zoo—I promise." I said as I arose to give him a hug, "You'll see—the penguins are fine."

"Daddy, you can't take me to the zoo if you're dead. You promised. You have to take me to the zoo again to save the penguins. You can't die. You can't die! We have to save the penguins. I don't want you to die!"

I woke up. No one was there. I jumped out of bed and searched the room. Michael was nowhere to be found. I checked the closet, and under the bed—no Michael. I sat down on the edge of the bed trembling and sweating. What just happened? I swear I saw Michael standing next to the bed. It was real. But where did he go? I needed a cigarette. I grabbed one from the pack I had on the chest along with my lighter. I checked the room again…no one there. Wide awake now, I put on my robe and slippers and walked downstairs. I went through the door and to the driveway. Looking up at the stars once again, I lit up. The vision of Michael had been so clear. How did he know I was about to die? I noticed a faint light coming from the back of the house. I peeked around the edge of the house and saw Sue's car parked in its usual spot. Curious as to where the light was coming from, I walked around back and saw Sue sitting in a chair on the small concrete patio in front of her door. The patio light was on and Sue sat beneath it smoking a cigarette. I didn't know Sue smoked. Talking to someone would help me clear my head of the manic confusion I was experiencing. I decided to visit with Sue. I was standing in the dark and she did not notice me right away. As I walked toward her I noticed that she had a glass next to her sitting on a small patio table. The short glass contained a brown liquid on ice. I didn't want to sneak up on her and frighten her, so I called out to her before she could see me.

"Hey Sue. Up kinda late huh?"

She jumped in her chair a little—I did scare her somewhat. Squinting to try and see me she asked, "Who's there?"

"Al—I couldn't sleep so I came out for a smoke and noticed your light on."

By the time I had finished talking, I was standing in front of her. Her face opened up into a wide smile as she gave me a loving look. Her eyes sparkled through her wire-rimmed glasses.

"Hey Sugar, what are you doing up so late?"

"I could be asking you the same question." I said

Sue let out a tired sigh. She was still dressed in her "Pancake Hut" uniform. Dark blue slacks, black tennis shoes, light blue short sleeve button down shirt still holding her name tag below her left shoulder, and a dark blue hair scarf holding back her gray hair. She looked exhausted but content.

"I just worked the evening shift and didn't get home long ago. I was supposed to be off all day, but one of the waitresses called in sick and they called me and asked if I would come in."

"You gotta work tomorrow?" I asked.

"No, thank God." She answered, "I'm glad I worked tonight, even though I am so tired. It was nice to do something a little different. You usually see the same people day after day when you work mornings. But tonight there were a lot of faces I had never seen before, not to mention a lot of drunks walked in when it got late. That made the night interesting."

I pictured the "Bernie's" crew walking in for an early breakfast to help them sober up. I always came straight home not wanting to risk a longer drive while driving intoxicated. Sue pointed to a chair on the other side of the table.

"Grab that chair and pull it over here under the light and have a seat."

I went over, picked up the chair and carried over and sat it against the house about four feet from Sue. I took a seat and leaned forward with my elbows on my knees.

"I didn't know you smoked." I said.

"This is the only cigarette I have during the day—one right before bed."

"Can I have one?" I asked having already extinguished the one I had come out with, and still a little shaken from my dream.

"Sure Honey. I'm guessing this is not your only one of the day." She said as she handed me the pack that was sitting on the table.

"No" I answered "This may make one pack for the day….If this is the only one you smoke during the day, can't you just quit?"

Sue gazed up toward the sky. She was smiling as she reached for her glass and took a sip looking upward.

"On nights like this my husband and I use to sit outside, just like we are now, and stare at the stars while we have a glass of bourbon and a cigarette."

"That's bourbon?" I asked as I nodded toward her glass.

"Yeah, I'm so sorry Sugar. I didn't even offer you any. You wanna glass?"

"Sure" I answered, not being one to ever turn down a free drink.

Sue started to get up. She was so tired that I felt guilty forcing her to have to get up from the spot where she seemed so comfortable. I stopped her.

"Don't get up. Just tell me where to find everything and I will get it myself."

"It's no problem Sugar, this is what I do. I enjoy taking care of people. You just sit there and I'll be right back."

I am sitting outside at 3:00 in the morning staring at a star-filled sky with a gray haired lady at least fifteen years my senior. I missed Flora even more at this point knowing that I should be experiencing this moment with her. Sue returned with my drink.

"Here ya go Honey." She said as she handed me the glass along with a napkin. It was short glass filled to the top with crushed ice and bourbon. "This is some good stuff—Maker's Mark".

"Thank you very much." I said as I carefully took the glass.

I took a sip, not wanting to shoot it all down at once as I was accustomed to.

Sue took her seat and leaned back. She returned her focus to the sky.

"But what you were saying about me quitting smoking," she continued, "at these times I can bring my husband back to me as I stare into the sky and do the things that we did together. I know that he is watching me from somewhere out there and it makes me feel secure. He's havin' a cigarette and a drink as he watches me. I talk to him and I listen intently for any messages he may have to give me. It may sound stupid but it's something I look forward to."

"Doesn't sound stupid at all." I said, "Am I interrupting this time for you? Would you like me to go so you can talk to him?"

"No Sugar. It's nice to have someone sitting with me. At least I can hear you when you talk to me."

"You ever hear him?" I asked.

"I don't hear him, but I can sometimes see signs that he is with me."

"Really? Like what?"

"Just one example—one night as I was talking to him, I was distressed and lonely, I said 'Sweetie, I feel as though I am wasting my time here talking to you. Can you really hear me?' I sat here waiting for an answer and got nothing. I went to bed thinking that my chats with him were useless. The next morning as I came out the door to leave for work, I looked down and saw four white feathers lying at the edge of the patio. The feathers were lined up perfectly, side by side, equal distances apart. Angels have white feathers. I was shocked. I started to cry. I went to pick up the feathers and a gust of wind came along at that time and picked them up into the air and they disappeared into the sky. How could they have blown onto my patio and lined themselves up so perfectly, before being blown away again? I was disappointed that they had gotten away from me, but I had to leave for work. I got into my car and as soon as I cranked it up the radio was playing the song 'Angel of the Morning'. I cried again. From that point on I knew that he was with me every second of every day. My time here talking to him is not a waste of time. He hears me."

Sue wiped a tear from her cheek though she was smiling. I felt as though she was glad to have me there with her. She wanted me to hear that story.

"That's amazing" I said.

Sue continued, "Did I ever tell you how I lost my Dick?"

"Excuse me?"

"Dick was my husband's name. Did I ever tell you how he died?"

"Oh…no."

"I'll give you the whole story unless you need to go to bed." She said before taking a sip from her glass.

"I'm not tired. I'm enjoying talking to you. Tell me a bedtime story." I said before taking a sip of my own.

I leaned back in my chair and crossed my legs. Sue sat her glass back down and leaned back in her chair. She put out her cigarette in the ash tray on the table and looked toward the sky.

"We got married when I was twenty-five and Dick was thirty-eight. He was a good bit older than me but he was so handsome and so sweet, I just knew he was the one for me. We wanted to have children but we found out after trying for a spell that I couldn't. I'm not gonna go into detail as to why. We were disappointed but we loved each other and our own company was good enough. Adoption was not an option. It wasn't that important to us. Dick was an insurance salesman. He hated being stuck in an office eight hours a day. But it paid the bills and then some, giving us a nice home to live in and allowing us to have and do pretty much anything we wanted to. What he really enjoyed was being outside and doing things around the house. When the storage area of our basement got full Dick built a storage shed out back; built it by himself with no help. When the storage shed got full he built a bigger storage building; in this one he included a workshop with a workbench so he could have a place to go outside the house when the weather was rough. It was complete with electricity, a bathroom and a refrigerator. He'd spend hours out there. He planted a garden every spring, he kept the lawn in perfect shape, and he planted flowers and shrubbery every year to add beauty to the landscaping. We never called a professional for any work to be done at home. Dick was an amateur electrician, plumber, heating and air man, carpenter, roofer, anything that needed to be done he did himself and did it well. He never complained either. I think he enjoyed having something break so that he would have the chance to fix it. And as I said before, at the end of the day we would sit outside, or inside during cold or rainy nights, and just enjoy each other's company. He made me feel as though all the hard work he did, at work and at home, was done so that we could enjoy those moments."

"Sounds like quite a man." I interjected.

"He was. But about five years ago, he went to the doctor because he was feelin' a lot of pain throughout his entire body. A doctor was a professional that he couldn't replace. After pokin' on him doin' all sorts of tests he was diagnosed with a degenerative bone disease that progressively took away his ability to do the things he loved doing. I couldn't even pronounce it. I just knew it was bad. As it got worse and worse he was forced into a wheelchair, only able to walk a few feet at a time."

"That's terrible. What did he do?" I asked.

"For a while he would still go outside on his little 'scooter' I called it. It got him around, even outside, pretty well. It was one of those little electric thingies. He would park it and get off of it to do little things like pick stuff from the garden or trim the bushes. But his movement got to be so limited that after a while he would just wander around outside on his scooter and sometimes sit and stare into space. I felt so bad for him. He was on all sorts of medication—most of it for pain. I had to hire someone to keep the lawn mowed, and he would sit and stare out the window watching the man cut the grass. I know that hurt him an awful lot."

Sue was now wiping away tears without the smile. I felt bad for forcing her into this emotional speech, but I felt that she wanted to tell me. She needed to talk to someone. This may have been the first time she had talked about him so openly since his death.

She continued, "One night we were sitting together in the living room watching TV. Dick asked me what we were having for dinner. I said, 'Sweetie we just had dinner. We had pork chops. Don't you remember?' He didn't. He had the strangest confused look on his face. The next day I drove to the drugstore to get his prescriptions filled. That night as we were lying in bed, he told me goodnight and kissed me like he had not kissed me in years. I thought that he was just feeling especially appreciative of me at that time. I got up the next morning and went into the kitchen to make breakfast. On the counter I saw one of the bottles of pills I had gotten for him the day before....It was empty. I ran back into the bedroom to wake Dick up but he wouldn't wake up. I shook him and shook him but he was gone."

"He.... killed himself?" I asked in a hushed voice.

Sue didn't answer right away. She got up and walked inside. She left the door open so I assumed she was returning. A few seconds later she came back out and sat down. She was sniffing. She had gone inside for some tissue. She wiped her face and blew her nose before continuing.

"Yes, he did. And do you know why?

"Why?"

Sue looked straight into my eyes and said, "Because he loved me."

She then started to cry more than just a teary eyed whimper. I got up from my seat and went to her. I put my hand behind her head and pulled her close to me. She wrapped her arms around my waist and pressed the side of her head to my stomach. She cried quietly. After a few moments she pulled away and blew her nose again. I returned to my chair.

"Because he loved you?" I asked.

"He thought that along with his physical disabilities, he would be nothing but a burden to me when senility was added. He didn't want me to be forced to take care of him and constantly watch over him. No, he didn't come out and tell me any of this, but I knew how he was thinking. His thought was that I was too young to be imprisoned with an invalid. I was mad at him for what he did at first. But it wasn't long before I realized that he did it for me, not selfishly.

And as much as I miss him, to this day, I can't fault him for what he did. He did it because he loved me."

"It doesn't anger you at all anymore?"

Sue focused on me with a serious look. She was no longer crying. She stared at me like a mother scolding a child.

"It would have angered me to no end if he had done it because things just weren't going his way. If it had been a way of just giving up on life I would have been pissed—you better believe it."

"Dick did not give up on life, he lived it to the fullest." She was still staring me down as if I had insulted her in some way. "He did it to protect me. Someone who takes their own life out of self-pity, I have absolutely nothing but contempt for—their cowards! You know why most people commit suicide?"

'Uh…no" I said, as if not knowing would bring me some sort of punishment.

"I don't either, but a lot of times it's because their girlfriend, boyfriend, husband, wife, whatever dumped 'em! Why kill yourself over the actions of somebody else? If that other person was perfect for you, you'd still be together!"

It started to seem as if Sue was talking about me. She was looking at me as if she knew what I had planned. She then pointed her finger directly at me.

"You may say, 'but she was perfect for me'—Bullshit! Couples, who are perfect for one another, like Dick and me, work through problems and stay together. Our lives weren't peaches and cream all the time, but we never even thought about splitting up. It wasn't an option. But when a split up does happen, no matter who makes the decision, it tells you that those two are not perfect for one another. If one is in love and the other has fallen out of love—where's the perfection? The one who has fallen out of love is the one with a real problem. You still have love inside of you and that's something to be proud of. There is someone out there that is perfect for you—find HER!"

I knew now that Sue was talking to me and about me. She continued to admonish me but softened her tone.

"Until you find her, start loving yourself. You are an intelligent, handsome loving man. I saw the love that surrounds you the first time we met—it's a gift I can't explain. Direct that love inward and start enjoying your own company. A lover is great to have, and you will have another, but until then know that your happiness comes from inside of you and not from somebody else!"

As I sat there, I was stunned by the lashing Sue had just given me. I looked at her not knowing what to say. How did she know? I sat in silence for a few seconds just absorbing the words thrown my way. And they were thrown like daggers. It was my turn to cry. I put my head in my hands and started sobbing. Sue got up from her chair and embraced me the same way I had embraced her minutes ago. I looked up at her. The love had returned to her eyes as she smiled down at me.

"How did you know?" I asked her.

"Dick told me—last night."

I pulled away from Sue and reached up to grab a white feather that had just landed on her shoulder.

~

I woke up the next morning at 8:20. It was Sunday and for
some reason I was extremely hungry. I had gotten very little sleep
but I got out of bed feeling well rested. I guess the nap I had taken
the previous afternoon helped provide me with the sleep I
needed. I put on a pair of jogging shorts and a t-shirt. I went
downstairs to look for something to eat. I could have grabbed a
granola bar or a banana, but I felt as though I needed something
more substantial. What the hell? I decided, 'I'm gonna cook
breakfast'. In the eight months I had lived here I had never even
touched the stove. I had used the microwave on occasion but had
never done any real cooking. Albert and Louise will be up soon.
I made the decision to cook breakfast for the whole house. Sue
was up past 4:00AM and would probably sleep in, but I wanted to
make sure there was enough just in case she was up soon. I had no
food in the refrigerator so a trip to the grocery store would be
required. I ran upstairs, put on my shoes, grabbed my wallet and
walked out the door.

I checked my wallet to see how much cash I had left. I still had
$93.00 of the $342.00 I had withdrawn a few days before. $249.00

had been spent on booze and cigarettes the previous two days and nights—I'm no financial wizard. I still had plenty to get all the fixings for a hearty breakfast.

As I drove to the store I thought about the previous night. Michael and Sue had shown me how selfish and uncaring I was being. Although Michael's input was in a dream, I believe his heart was in the room with me. Michael deserves to grow up with a real father and I know that he does not want me to go away. He loves me and I have to take him to the zoo—the penguins are in trouble. Sue, through her remarkable intuition and contact with the hereafter, knew of my intentions. She is an amazing, caring woman and knew exactly where to be last night in order to get her message to me. Dick is apparently an amazing and caring spirit. I was in no way cured from my loneliness and depression, but I knew that dying was not going to solve anything. My Monday plan to become a corpse was cancelled. All safety measures would be adhered to as I unloaded the freight. I repeated to myself along the drive, "I want to live". I had spent the last few months hating myself and starting to love myself, as Sue had suggested, would be something I would have to work on. I thought I could start by being nicer to others and giving them a reason to love me as well. Providing breakfast for my housemates would be a step in that direction.

I arrived back home with several bags of groceries. Included in the bags were two cans of tuna to replace the tainted ones in the cabinet. I took them in and sat them on the kitchen counter. As I started to unload the bags I looked out the back window and saw Sue, dressed in her robe, grabbing the newspaper from her patio. I opened the window and got her attention.

"Hey" I yelled.

Sue looked around, not knowing where the voice was coming from.

"Up here—kitchen window." I shouted.

Sue looked up to the window and saw me waving.

"Good morning, Honey" she said, "How you feelin'?"

"Good" I answered, "Come up for breakfast in forty-five minutes."

"You cookin'?"

"Yeah, forty-five minutes—okay?"

"Okay Dear."

Sue then gave me a smile and went back inside. I was glad that she was up. I had the chance to do something nice for her, although I would never be able to repay her for what she had done for me. It was 9:15 on Sunday morning and I then realized that I was yelling out the window from inside the house. If I had awakened Louise she might have killed me anyway. Louise usually visited her sister on Sundays and Albert went to church on Sunday mornings. I believe he attended "Saint Lucifer's Church of Fat Assholes" (Oh yeah, I'm suppose to start being nice). They were usually both up before 10:00. Neither of these two had been my most favorite person over the last several months, but I wanted to do something good for them. I had to live with them so I wanted to attempt to make things a little more amicable between us. I'm sure that I had not been one of their favorites either. I was always in a hurry to get away from them whenever our paths crossed.

I made the breakfast that I had made for others many times before. During my marriage and my time with Flora I did most of the cooking because I enjoyed it. But Sunday morning breakfast was the most special and enjoyable. It was a day in which everyone could sleep late, stay in our pajamas all day and be as lazy as we wanted to be. I usually had it ready between 10:30 and 11:00, that way no one had to get up too early to enjoy it. After we ate I would read the Sunday paper, do the crossword and then lie on the couch and scratch while I watched whatever sport was in season on TV. Everyone else would also do as they pleased—nap, play outside, lay in the sun, computer, whatever. Sunday is "the day of rest" and that is what we did.

I cooked up a dozen scrambled eggs and added some chunks of cheese to melt in with them, fried sausage links, bacon, biscuits (yes, homemade), fried cubed potatoes, and I cut up a fresh cantaloupe. After everything was ready I set the table with everything else needed to complete the spread—grape jelly, strawberry preserves, ketchup, hot sauce, and orange juice. I made a pot of real coffee—not instant, not decaf.

As I was emptying the eggs into a serving bowl Louise walked into the kitchen. She gave me a confused look. She had never seen me at the stove before. She looked at the food and condiments on the table and smiled.

"You made breakfast." She said in a high pitched voice, "How sweet."

"It's ready." I said, "Have a seat. Want some coffee?"

"Are you serious?" she asked, "You made breakfast for everyone?"

"Yeah, I had to use up all this food today. The expiration date on all of it is tomorrow." I joked.

"Yes, on the coffee." She said as she sat, "This looks great Al."

I poured her a cup of coffee and sat it in front of her.

"Forgot to put out the cream and sugar" I said, "Let me grab it."

As I pulled the cream from the refrigerator Sue walked in.

"Mornin' guys" she said as she eyed the food on the table. "This looks wonderful Al. I can't wait to get at it. It's nice to have someone else serve you instead of having to serve people you don't know. I tip well—just so ya know."

"Cash only" I said "The credit card machine is down."

Sue didn't waste any time. She sat down and started loading up her plate.

"Coffee?" I asked her.

"Yes, please."

I got Sue her coffee and then sat down to join them. After fifteen minutes or so, Albert came walking downstairs—nothing but shorts on, of course. I was glad that I was almost finished. However the sight and smell of Albert made me wonder if my food was going to stay down.

"Mornin' Albert."

"Mornin' Albert."

"Mornin' Albert."

We took turns greeting the walrus. His response was a grunt....literally no words were formed. He waddled over to the refrigerator, opened it and started scanning the shelves. I watched him along with Louise and Sue. He was extremely gross to look at but the sight was just too fascinating to look away. He scratched his butt and then grabbed the milk with the same hand (If Albert offers you milk, say "no").

Finally I said, "Albert I made breakfast. There's plenty here."

He turned and looked at the spread on the table. Wide-eyed, he put the milk back in the refrigerator.

"Really?" He asked, "Damn, looks good."

He then waddled over to the table, sat down and loaded up his plate. I took that to be his "thank you".

"Well, enjoy" I said as I excused myself, "I'm gonna take a shower and then go for a walk."

"It was delicious, Dear." Said Sue.

"Very good" said Louise.

Albert just chewed. I smiled and walked upstairs. I showered, got dressed and was leaving my room as Albert walked by, having finished his breakfast.

"Thank you." He said with a rare smile, "That was the best meal I have had in a long time. I never cook for myself and I have no one else to do it for me. I really appreciate it."

I had no idea Albert was able to string that many words together audibly. He had always been gruff and surly, speaking few words. I had never seen this side of him. Maybe he was an asshole to me because he thought that I had been an asshole to him—quite possible that I had been. Anyway, I could tell that he was being genuine with his words and was appreciative.

"Happy to do it." I said as I patted him on his bare back. I returned to the bathroom to wash my hands and then descended the stairs.

I had put on a pair of khaki cargo shorts and a yellow t-shirt. I wore my sneakers for the walk. It was a little overcast out, but I knew that the sun would probably be out soon. It was unusually cool for a June morning—maybe sixty-five degrees.

I felt a little chilly at first but knew the walk would warm me up. I chose to walk into town. It was close and I had never done it before. I had always driven. The streets of Pyeville were beautiful. The old houses and their nicely manicured and landscaped yards gave me a very pleasant view as I strode the sidewalk. There were many others out on foot—some running, some walking their dog, some pushing baby strollers. I saw one industrious woman doing all three. I heard church bells in the distance….yeah, it's almost 11:00—time for God. Instead of going to church I thought that I would just invite God to go for a walk with me on this Sunday. And if God has anything to say to me…I'm listening.

Of course my thoughts drifted to Flora as I walked the tree-lined streets. Our lives had changed drastically over the past eight months. Raymond was gone now but there was still no room in her life for me. The death of a loved one changes people and it definitely had changed Flora as well as her children. I think that she had put aside all of her reasons for divorcing Raymond when he moved back in with them. That left her with the love she had had for him when they were first married. That made her a grieving widow now, and grieving widows do not immediately pick up where they left off with past relationships. Our talks had dwindled down from every day in the beginning to not at all. It had been over two months since our last contact when she called me to inform me of Raymond's passing. At the time Flora asked me to move out so that Raymond could move back in, I almost asked her if I could move back in after he died. That question had now been answered—no. I knew that the kids never wanted to see me again. They felt cheated because I had taken too much of their mom's time and also had taken up the space once occupied by their dad. They felt as though they had lost time with each because of me. I held no ill feelings for these children. They are good kids and did not deserve to go through this type of "hell" at such a young age. Flora, I now knew, also did not want me back. I still loved her and wanted her back but I had accepted the fact that it was not going to happen. This was not fair to Flora either. I knew that she still loved me and in her perfect world we would still be together. But in the grief that surrounded her and the kids, I would not fit in. They needed each other's love and support, not my intrusion.

As I got closer to town the sidewalk got more crowded. The people that were passing me were actually smiling at me—some even said "hello". Perhaps that aura of love was surrounding me again. It wasn't my love for another, but my newfound love for life and a growing love for myself. I had even gained a soft spot for Albert. I realized now that my previous feelings of being cheated out of my relationship with Flora were valid. I was forced to leave someone that I loved dearly for reasons out of my control and not because of anything I had done. But no one was to blame.

Everyone involved did what was right. However, the outcome—death, grief, and a break-up—made it a no-win situation for all involved. While my feelings of being cheated were valid, I did act selfishly. Sometimes doing what's right hurts, and the urge to do what's wrong wins out because it is more comfortable. Flora forced me into doing what was right even though I wanted the comfort of remaining with her and the kids. I looked skyward and mentally apologized to Raymond. In all of my previous thoughts I had failed to have any sympathy for a man who had lost his life. Those of us still here had to deal with that loss, but at least we were still here. I could continue to hope that Flora and I would be together again one day, stupidly in love and enjoying every second together. I cannot depend on that. But no matter whom I may end up with, Flora will always own the biggest chunk of my heart.

I arrived into town as the sun was beginning to shine in full force. I had no plan of what to do when I got there. Most of the businesses in town were closed on Sunday but I noticed quite a few cars parked in the streets. Oh yeah… "Bernie's" opens at eleven on Sunday for brunch—one of their busiest days from what I hear. I decided that as long as I was here I would walk in for a beer. In fact I could have as many as I wanted because I had walked and wouldn't have to drive home. I headed down the sidewalk in that direction and as "Bernie's came into view I noticed a small crowd of folks standing at the front door. As I got closer I could see that it was Sid, Giblet, and three people I did not know. The three strangers, two men and a woman, were dressed nicely—probably had just attended an early church service. I had never been to the bar this early in the day and I suspected that it would be full of families enjoying brunch—most likely not a very wild crowd. Kids were not common in "Bernie's" normally, but I was sure they would be here today. We would probably have to watch the language. Baptists, kids and cussing don't blend well together. Sid saw me as I was just a few yards away. He smiled and raised his hand in a wave. He yelled out to me,

"Goddamn, look who came in on a Sunday mornin' for a bloody fuckin' mary."

He then laughed just as loud as he had yelled; so much for watching the language. The lady standing with the other two gentlemen turned and looked at Sid as if he had used the "f" word and taken the Lord's name in vain. I was almost embarrassed to acknowledge that I knew him. The lady turned back toward the other two men with a look of disgust and rolled her eyes. Sid was not able to see her roll her eyes but had noticed that she was not happy with his greeting toward me. Sid walked over to her.

"Maam, I'm sorry for my language." He said in a very apologetic voice.

The lady forced a smile and said, "That's okay."

Sid is a large, well built man, and toward over the trio. The other two men smiled nervously and then the three nicely dressed smokers stepped on their cigarettes and headed inside. As they opened the door and were about to enter Sid said to them,

"Ya'll enjoy ya fuckin' brunch."

I had reached the restaurant front in time to witness Sid's apology and well wishes.

"Hey Sid, Gib" I said as I took a seat on the bench and lit a cigarette. Both Sid and Giblet stood in front of me. I was tired from my walk and needed to sit.

"Never seen ya here this early" said Giblet, "You gonna watch the race with us? Starts at one."

"Yeah" said Sid, "We gonna watch the race and have some eggs fuckin' benedict." He then laughed again.

"Did you start drinkin' at home this mornin'?" I asked Sid, "They've only been open thirty minutes and it looks like you're already close to your limit."

"Whataya mean did I start at home?" he asked, "You have to stop before you can start and I ain't stopped since last night. Lori'll let me know when I've had enough…. Ya know how she does that?"

Giblet and I both shook our heads.

"She wakes me up and tells me to get up outa the yard and get in the fuckin' house." Sid followed that statement with another hearty laugh.

Giblet asked me again, "You gonna watch the race with us?"

"Not much of a race fan Gib" I answered, "I'm gonna come in for a beer or two though."

"You don't like NASCAR?" Giblet asked.

"No, got nothing against it or anybody that wants to watch it. I just never got into it."

"Cuz you're a goddamn pussy." Said Sid as he looked at me.

"I may be a pussy but I'm not gonna be throwing up in my front yard tonight." I said.

"Me neither" said Sid as if I had insulted him. "I'll be throwin' up long before night." He laughed again as he bent over and slapped me on the shoulder.

Jan walked out of the bar and lit a cigarette. She saw me and immediately walked over and sat on the bench beside me. She was wearing tight blue short shorts and an even tighter white tank top. The cleavage ran from her chin to her naval.

"Hey Sweetie" she said, "you gonna come in for a beer and watch the race with us?"

"He don't like NASCAR." Sid said in a nya nya voice.

"No" I said, "I'm not a fan. But I'm comin' in for a drink."

Jan then leaned closer to me so the other two couldn't hear and asked me, "Why don't we go to my house after the race for drinks and more?"

A day or two earlier the answer to that question would have

been an emphatic "yes". I wasn't sure how to answer at this time, but fortunately before I had a chance to respond Sid leaned down with his head between ours and asked, "Ya'll talkin' bout me?"

"Yeah" I said, "Jan just told me you had a teeny dick."

"How does she know?" He asked as he stood up straight, "She's never seen it."

"I talk to Lori a lot." Jan said, "Sometimes she gets a little tipsy and starts tellin' secrets."

"She's never complained to me before." Sid responded, "She always seems to be satisfied."

"That's cuz I'm doin' her on the side." Said Giblet, "I'm the one keepin' her satisfied."

"Why are you doin' her on the side?" Sid asked, "I just usually do her from behind."

That got a laugh from everyone—Sid was loudest of course. Rod walked out of the door and saw that everyone had been amused.

"What's so funny?" he asked.

"Sid's got a little dick." Jan answered still laughing.

"Yeah, I know." Said Rod, "That's why I make him wear three rubbers."

Rod then noticed me for the first time. "Sup Al? You gonna come in and watch the ra......?"

I interrupted him, "No! I don't like NASCAR! If ya'll wanna sit and watch cars goin' around in circles…"

"Ovals" Giblet interrupted.

"Ovals….whatever—passing each other without once using their blinkers that's fine. I'll sit and watch one of the other TV's while I drink my beer—maybe a bowling tournament, women's golf, the history of disposable diapers—ANYTHING BUT NASCAR!"

The "Neverlaid Brothers" had walked up to enter the bar as I was completing my mock tirade. Dressed in their polyester shorts, plaid button down shirts, and sandals accompanied with white socks they stood alongside the rest of the group.

Phil looked at Don and asked, "You ever had sex in a car?"
"No" Don answered. He then looked over to Jan and asked. "Jan, what's it like to have sex in a car?"
"Why are you two concerned?" she asked, "You can't have sex in a mo ped."
Everyone had extinguished their cigarettes so I walked to the door and opened it. I held it open and motioned for the rest of the gang to come in. They walked by me and through the door one by one, still laughing at Jan's jab. She was the last one through and stopped in the doorway to ask me, "Well? Whataya think?" Still waiting for an answer to her previous invitation.
I looked down at her and smiled.
"We'll see." I said.
She smiled, kissed me on the cheek and continued in. After everyone had entered I stood at the door, still holding it open, and looked inside. Nathan, Bobby and Gino were sitting at the bar. Sid and Giblet took their seats beside them. Rod sat next to Frank on the opposite side of the bar. Jan joined Paula and Jerry who were having brunch in a booth. A few short months ago I had been lonely and without a friend. I had grown to love these people. I had grown to depend on them to be here every time I arrived and they usually were. What had begun as a lonely visit into a strange place had become a return home to family. We laughed, we cried on one another's shoulders, we traded jabs, we hugged, we drank.
Stephanie was behind the bar pouring drinks. Along with Joanie, Merilyn, Bonnie and Jenny she took care of me like a doting wife wanting to keep her man happy. They made sure my

glass was never empty, my food was always hot, and on those rare occasions that I was at the bar without a friend to talk to, they kept me company until a friend arrived. They always offered to call me a cab if they thought that I had had too much.

And Joanie even gave me a ride of her own once—in more ways than one.

Randy was standing at the end of the bar. He was looking over the entire place just to make sure things were going smoothly. As much as I had disliked Randy and the rudeness he exhibited at times, I felt no ill will toward him. This was his place, he hired the people that took care of me, and his doors were open for my friends and me every day. His place gave me a spot to visit and make new friends when I was at the lowest point of my life. I felt at home with this entire group. Not only did I need them, they made me feel as if they needed me.

Despite this realization, I remained outside the door unable to enter. I didn't want this anymore. The people inside, who I cared about very much, were not who I wanted to be. I do not want to be sitting on a barstool at "Bernie's", when I am sixty-years-old, greeting people by name as they walk through the door. I could not continue to sit and get drunk every night, watching TV with my elbows parked on the bar. If that is what the others want to do and it makes them happy—great. I need more. I want to have someone at home with me to love—someone I can't wait to wake up with in the morning and come home to in the evening. Not someone I have to get away from by coming to a bar. I am never going to have this if I continue what I am doing. If my buddies want to play golf, go to dinner (somewhere other than "Bernie's"), attend a movie, or go to a game, I'll be excited to do that. I wanted to do things that did not involve getting polluted every night. It had become time to stop. The separation from

Flora had been unbelievably difficult. Could I handle a separation from "Bernie's"? I had to find out.

"You comin' in?" Nathan yelled at me from the bar.

I looked around and saw that everyone was waiting on my response.

"No" I said, "I gotta go."

I waved to everyone and let the door close as I retreated back outside.

~

I backed away from the front door and turned to continue my walk. I stopped in front of the jewelry store and stood to admire the wooden cane that remained attached to the building. No one had tampered with it and apparently Randy's heart had softened enough to allow it to remain. I guess no one wanted to be the one to disrespect an old man who was no longer with us. Charlie had been a lucky man. Despite his usual ornery demeanor, he had run his business successfully for over forty years and remained married to his wife for over fifty years. His family loved him, his town loved him and he had provided well for both. He left a valuable business for his kids to continue or sell. Either way, his children will not be mowing their own lawns. I considered contacting his son, David, and asking about the job of running the store—could be profitable for me. Charlie passed the bar when he was twenty-one years old. I just passed a bar for what seems to be the first time since I was twenty-one.

I walked past the jewelry store and followed the sidewalk past the beauty salon and real estate office—both closed. The sun was shining brightly but the awnings that covered the storefronts

shielded my eyes from it. The temperature had risen since I had
left the house. It was now around eighty degrees. A few people
were scattered along the sidewalk but not many. I approached the
antique store where I had bought the cane for Charlie's mini
memorial. The store was open but I saw no one inside. I stopped
to peer inside the display window. An old 'Radio Flyer' wagon
was the centerpiece of the display. I don't think I have ever seen
an antique store without an old red wagon. Around the wagon
was an old washboard, a mini grandfather clock, a portable record
player, a gun holster complete with guns, a small stand-up
microphone, a moonshine jug and some other small items. Inside
the wagon sat a porcelain doll, a 'Raggedy Ann'' doll, and some
comic books leaning against the side. I wanted to go in but knew
that if I did I would end up with something I don't need, like a
butter mold or an eighty-year-old dildo labeled as a back
massager. I continued to walk.

I reached the corner and looked to the opposite side of the
street. I had never paid attention much to this area because the bar
is the only place I visited in town. I noticed a store that had
'Carla's New and Used Books' scripted across the window. I
thought that a book would be something that may help to keep
me out of the bar. I decided to cross the street and see if it was
open. As I moved from under the awning the sun was staring
straight at me as I faced my target. I could not see the crossing
indicator or the cars on the street. After making the decision to
remain among the living, I did not want to step in front of an
unseen vehicle. A man wearing sunglasses walked up next to me
and waited to proceed to the other side. I thought I would just
cross when he crossed. As long as he is not suicidal I should be
okay. After a few moments he stepped onto the street so I just
followed behind him. As I reached the other side I noticed that
the store had an 'OPEN' sign on the door. I walked inside and

was immediately greeted by a voice from someone I could not see.

"Hi. How are you today?" It was a woman's voice.

"I'm fine." I said, "You?"

Having just come out of the bright sunshine, my eyes had not yet adjusted to the dimmer lighting inside the store. I could make out a figure behind the counter but it was dark and yellow spots surrounded it. The counter was against the left wall at the front of the store. I could tell that the walls were lined with shelves around the entire perimeter. As I walked toward the counter I was able to slowly start focusing on my greeter.

"I'm very good." She said, "Is there anything I can help you find?"

Just as she had finished her question, the image began to get clearer. She was sitting on a stool behind the counter, legs crossed, holding an open book in her lap. It was the same woman that had caught me singing the "Happy Days" theme at work. She was gorgeous. The musty smell of an old building and worn books faded as I neared her and detected her heavenly aroma. She looked directly at me, smiling and waiting for my response. I was hoping that she did not recognize me. Our first meeting had been very embarrassing for me.

"No thanks" I said, "I'm just gonna browse."

I wanted to stand there in front of her and admire her beauty. She had shoulder length brunette hair that was held back on one side and fell freely on the other, big blue eyes, dark smooth skin, and a kindness in her smile I had only witnessed once before. She wore a dark blue golf shirt with a logo of the bookstore under her left shoulder, and white shorts. She was dressed for a Sunday at work. Although she sat I remembered watching her walk away from me that day at work. Her body told me she was twenty-five, but a slight indication of lines around her eyes told me she was forty. The hint of lines did nothing to take away from her beauty. There was no ring on her left ring finger. It was facing toward me as she held her book. I saw her much differently on this day. For the first time since I first met Flora, I was smitten by the sight of a woman.

"Browse all you want." She said, her eyes casting a spell on me, "My name's Carla. Yell if you need anything."

All I could do was smile and nod as I turned away from the counter and moved toward the bookshelves that lined the walls beside her. As I walked away I could hear her singing to herself in a soft voice, "Sunday Monday happy days". I turned back to see her giving me a mischievous grin. Embarrassed again, I smiled and continued toward the books.

There was no one in the place except for the two of us. Did I really say "browse"? Couldn't I have come up with something a little more manly like "look around" or "scope it out", or "Will you marry me and let me suck your toes?" I tried to focus on finding a book. I enjoy reading sports stories so I went to the shelves that were labeled 'SPORTS'. I browsed…uh looked at the titles on the shelf with my head turned sideways so I could read them as they stood upright.

Boxing? No….

Hockey? No….

NASCAR? Hell no!!!

Poker?… Poker's a sport? No….

Football? Now I can start browsing…uh looking. I flipped through a few books not finding anything interesting enough to purchase. I scanned the baseball, basketball, and sports biographies books and found nothing I wanted or haven't already read. As I flipped through one last book I took a peek toward Carla just to get another glimpse.

Still holding the book, I found myself staring at her, enamored by her splendor. I could now see her through the opening at the side of the counter. I was now maybe twenty feet away from her, but able to see her from head to toe. Her legs were dark and smooth, still femininely crossed, just like the rest of her complexion that I saw from the front of the counter. She wore white sandals, playing with one using her toes to tap it against her heel as she read. She looked up toward me and saw that I was looking at her. She gave me another kind smile. Embarrassed, I returned to the book I was holding, giving it my attention for a few seconds before placing it back on the shelf. Her name is the same name on the store window. Assuming that she owns the place, I had to find something to buy—as much as possible. Nothing makes a better first impression than helping make someone's business more profitable.

Unable to find anything that I wanted in the area where I was standing, I moved to the front of the store to check out the books displayed on tables near the front door and in front of the counter—also much closer to Carla. I approached a table and picked up a book, not paying attention to its title. The book was not my reason for being in this spot. I just wanted to be able to experience her scent again. I looked down at the banner that hung below the table. It read 'DIET BOOKS'. I could see Carla smiling, as she read, out of the corner of my eye. I was too embarrassed to look at her. She had either come to an amusing part of her book or was able to sense my discomfort for nosing through a diet book. I quickly sat the book down and moved to another table a little closer to the counter. 'Poetry' was on the banner that hung from this table. Poetry's not bad. I'll let her know that I have a sensitive side. I randomly picked up one of the poetry books and opened it. The page where I opened to was near the end of the book. I just read the first poem I saw.

"There are times in our life when only happiness is known and the future is our friend

When we know that the sun will shine bright on our dreams and this pleasure will never end

There are no dark clouds no misery or pain and all of our wants are met

No hunger of physical or spiritual needs, a bountiful table is set

But know that life's journey is not a straight path. There are detours, turns and twists

The future that we thought would bring us great joy contains heartache, grief, and no bliss

Don't wallow in sorrow, self-pity, and despair. Don't dwell on what you once had

There are no mistakes in our life's journey. There is a purpose in the good and the bad

So hold the reins loosely, prepared for the turns and continue determined and undaunted

The path may show that your previous dreams were not what you really wanted"

I paused for a few moments to absorb the words I had read. I read the poem again. After reading it a third time I continued to stare down at the page not wanting to look up. I was afraid that I would reveal tear-filled eyes. I turned and wiped each eye with a swipe of the back of my hand.

When I knew that there was no evidence of my emotions on my face, I looked up to see Carla now staring at me.

She smiled....I smiled.

God's talking and I'm listening.

I closed the book.... I'll get this one.

CPSIA information can be obtained at www.ICGtesting.com
Printed in the USA
LVOW061032201112

308043LV00001B/62/P